The Smuggler's Secrets

A Caroline Mystery

by Kathleen Ernst

★ American Girl®

Published by American Girl Publishing
Copyright © 2015 American Girl

Questions or comments? Call 1-800-845-0005,
visit **americangirl.com**, or write to Customer Service,
American Girl, 8400 Fairway Place, Middleton, WI 53562.

Printed in China
15 16 17 18 19 20 21 LEO 10 9 8 7 6 5 4 3 2 1

This book is a work of fiction. Any similarity to real persons, living or dead,
is coincidental and not intended by American Girl. References to real events,
people, or places are used fictitiously. Other names, characters, places, and
incidents are the products of imagination.

Cover image by Juliana Kolesova

The following individuals and organizations have given permission to use
images incorporated into the cover design: background pattern on back cover,
© kristypargeter/Crestock.

Cataloging-in-Publication Data available from the Library of Congress

For Stephanie

Beforever™

The adventurous characters you'll meet in
the BeForever books will spark your curiosity
about the past, inspire you to find your voice
in the present, and excite you about your future.
You'll make friends with these girls as you share
their fun and their challenges. Like you, they are
bright and brave, imaginative and energetic,
creative and kind. Just as you are, they are
discovering what really matters: Helping others.
Being a true friend. Protecting the earth.
Standing up for what's right. Read their stories,
explore their worlds, join their adventures.
Your friendship with them will BeForever.

TABLE *of* CONTENTS

chapter 1

Trouble on the Road

CAROLINE ABBOTT LOOKED over her shoulder as the wagon lurched away from Sackets Harbor. Away from *home*. From her perch on the wagon seat, she could see the roof of her house and the towering masts of navy ships anchored in the harbor. Beyond the familiar village, Lake Ontario was dappled with August sunshine. A cool breeze blew ashore.

Right this minute, she thought, *Papa is probably giving directions to the workers at the shipyard.* Caroline imagined Mama perched on a tall stool in the family shipyard office, checking a ledger. And it was baking day at home, so Grandmother was likely mixing bread dough. Caroline missed them already.

"Whoa, there," Uncle Aaron called to the white

1

horse hitched to the wagon. As the wagon halted, he smiled kindly at Caroline. "Take a good look."

"It must seem silly that I want to," Caroline said. After all, she would be home again in a few weeks.

"It's not silly at all," Uncle Aaron assured her.

Caroline admitted, "I will miss the lake." She dearly loved sailing Lake Ontario's restless water—especially in the little skiff her father had built.

"We know you miss your home when you stay at our farm," Lydia told her. Lydia Livingston was Caroline's cousin—and one of her best friends, too.

"I wish we didn't have to ask for your help again," Uncle Aaron added.

"You see, the neighbor men have been going from farm to farm, working together," Lydia said. "They'll be burning brush at our farm three days from now, and I can't manage all the cooking alone."

"Lydia has extra chores to do while I'm helping our neighbors, too," Uncle Aaron added.

Caroline could almost hear her grandmother's

voice: *Gracious, my girl. Are you going to mope about, or are you going to ease your uncle's and cousin's burdens?*

Caroline took one last look at Sackets Harbor. Then she turned to face the road ahead and lifted her chin. "I'm happy to help you at the farm," she assured them. "Let's go."

Until recently, Uncle Aaron, Aunt Martha, and Caroline's cousins Lydia and Oliver had lived on the northern shore of Lake Ontario, in the British colony of Upper Canada. With hard work, they'd established a good farm. But now the United States and Great Britain were at war. Lydia's family had fled enemy territory, leaving their livestock, crops, tools, furniture, and other valuables behind.

Now the Livingstons were struggling to create a new home in New York State's deep woods. Since Lydia's brother Oliver was helping the U.S. Navy fight the British, getting the farmwork done was harder than ever. Uncle Aaron had never complained about having to start over with almost nothing, but when Aunt Martha had been called away to tend a sick relative earlier that summer, Lydia had needed to take over all of the cooking and cleaning. Caroline had gone to the farm to help out. She'd been able to go home for a short visit, but now Uncle Aaron and Lydia had come to fetch her again.

"I'm glad you two could come for me," she said. Last time, she'd traveled with an elderly couple, Mr. and Mrs. Sinclair, who lived near Lydia. "Although it was kind of the Sinclairs to fetch me before," she added quickly.

"The Sinclairs loaned me their horse and wagon for this trip," Uncle Aaron explained. "I needed to visit Sackets Harbor myself this time. I'd hoped to buy an ox."

They passed out of the hot sunshine into the shady woods, and Lydia pushed her bonnet back. "Papa needs an ox to help work the farm," she said.

Caroline knew that any cattle trained for heavy labor were called oxen. Woodsmen used oxen to haul logs to her family's shipyard, and she had often marveled at the animals' strength. "Can Minerva help you?" she asked. Minerva and her calf, Garnet, were the Livingstons' cows. Caroline was quite fond of them.

"Minerva wasn't trained for the yoke," Lydia told her. "Besides, Minerva's most important jobs are to keep producing milk and to have another calf in the spring."

Uncle Aaron waved away a fly. "A few months ago, I sold my gold watch so that I could buy a young ox. Unfortunately, the price of oxen was higher than I'd expected."

"We'd hoped we could earn the difference by selling milk and butter," Lydia said.

"But you still don't have enough money to afford an ox?" Caroline asked.

Uncle Aaron looked glum. "Now there's not an animal to be had anywhere, at any price."

"Farmers in Upper Canada don't have enough

animals to feed all the troops that have arrived since the war began," Lydia said. "So the British are offering high prices for American beef. Cattle have been smuggled to Upper Canada all along the border."

"Wretched smugglers!" Caroline exclaimed. "Shame on them for helping our enemies." She simply could not understand how any American could sell food to the enemy! Her family would never help the British. When the war began a little over a year earlier, British sailors had captured Caroline's father and stolen a beautiful sloop he'd built. Papa had been held prisoner for a long time, and might *still* be a prisoner if he hadn't managed to escape. Caroline had wondered and worried about him for many long months. It had been *awful*.

"Smuggling is wicked," Lydia agreed.

"I understand your feelings," Uncle Aaron told them. "But it's a complicated situation. Some smugglers are poor farmers who desperately need the money they earn to survive."

Caroline was not convinced. *Uncle Aaron would never trade with our enemy,* she thought, even though she knew he worried about keeping his own farm going. That meant it was more important than ever that she help out while Aunt Martha was away. "I know your farm will be a success," she said stoutly.

Uncle Aaron patted her knee. "We'll manage somehow."

Caroline hated seeing him and Lydia troubled. She had a surprise for Lydia hidden in her valise, but she needed something to lift their spirits right now. She thought a moment before asking, "Do you remember the time Garnet knocked me over while I was trying to feed her?"

"Milk sprayed all over!" Lydia snickered. "You tried *so* hard not to lose your balance that you looked like you were dancing a silly jig."

"And remember when you let Minerva eat wild leeks?" Uncle Aaron grinned too. "You didn't know any better, Caroline, but oh my, her milk tasted like onions for a week!"

Caroline, Lydia, and Uncle Aaron shared more memories as they traveled farther west. "It's good to hear you girls giggling together again," Uncle Aaron said. The worried lines in his face had smoothed out, and he looked happy. That made Caroline happy too.

She held on to that feeling as they jolted deeper and deeper into the woods. Huge trees towered above the rutted dirt road, creating a dim world. It was a very different landscape than she saw at home, where the open sky and lake were always in view! They were traveling in roughly the same direction as the lakeshore, but they'd come far enough inland that Caroline couldn't catch even a glimpse of the water.

There were no villages in these deep woods, just a few scattered farms. The smell of smoke let her know when they were approaching a clearing. Faint whiffs hinted at small fires built by women doing laundry or cooking supper. Big plumes of smoke rose where

farmers were burning trees they'd chopped down
to clear new fields.

The wagon rounded a bend, and Caroline saw
a fire crackling along the edge of a clearing beside
the road. A billowing cloud of smoke threatened to
swallow them.

The horse stopped and whinnied nervously.
"Walk on, Snowflake," Uncle Aaron called. He jiggled
the lines encouragingly. "Come on, girl."

Caroline watched the white mare prance in place.
"Did the Sinclairs get a new horse?" she asked. "They
drove a calm, dark horse named Bess when I traveled
with them."

"They sold Bess and purchased Snowflake just last
week," Uncle Aaron told her. "Snowflake is skittish.
I'll have to lead her through." He handed the lines to
Lydia and climbed down from the wagon. After mur-
muring encouragement to Snowflake and patting her
neck, he was able to tug her into the smoke.

Lydia pulled a handkerchief from her pocket

and held it over her mouth and nose. "I should have warned you to have a handkerchief handy," she said.

Caroline remembered packing a handkerchief, but there was no time to dig through her valise for it. She closed her eyes against the smoke.

Uncle Aaron coughed several times, but soon enough the air improved. "There, now," he called. "We're through the worst of—" His sentence broke. "Girls, get into the back of the wagon," he said sharply.

Caroline's eyes flew open. Through tendrils of drifting smoke, she saw a horse-drawn cart loaded with barrels stopped in the road ahead, facing them. Several men stood around the cart, their hats pulled down low and kerchiefs tied over their faces so that only their eyes showed. Caroline froze when she saw that the men held muskets. The guns were pointed at the cart driver.

"Girls!" Uncle Aaron hissed over his shoulder. "Get into the back and lie down—*now*!"

chapter 2
Smugglers!

CAROLINE AND LYDIA scrambled over
the seat and landed in the wagon bed. Lydia still held
the lines leading to Snowflake, but Caroline grabbed
her cousin's free hand. "Are those men robbing the
driver?" she whispered.

Lydia's eyes were wide. "I think so!"

Uncle Aaron had told the girls to lie down, but
Caroline wanted badly to see what was happening.
She rose up on her elbows and peeked through the
gap under the seat.

The dark-haired man driving the cart was sitting
very straight and tall. "Be on your way!" he yelled
angrily to the men holding guns.

A robber who had a very long gray beard
shook his head. "We will *not*!" he retorted. "Not

until we get what we came for."

Caroline bit her lip, wondering what would happen next. She watched Uncle Aaron, who still stood beside Snowflake, take a deep breath and square his shoulders. "Good afternoon!" he called in friendly fashion. "What seems to be the trouble?"

"This doesn't concern you," the bearded man shouted. He seemed to be in charge of the thieves. "Just stay back there while we take care of business."

"That isn't a good idea." Uncle Aaron's hands were clenching and unclenching, but he managed to keep his voice calm. "I'm sure if you just—"

The lead robber swung his musket to his shoulder so fast that Caroline heard the shot crack the air before she'd realized what he was doing. Instinctively she dropped back to the floor of the wagon box.

"Papa!" Lydia shrieked.

"I'm all right, girls," Uncle Aaron called. "That shot was just a warning, aimed high. We'll stay right here until those men go on their way."

Caroline strained her ears for the sound of another shot. Finally she dared peep out again. Uncle Aaron still stood with his back to her, holding Snowflake's harness, watching the robbers.

The bearded man's musket was pointed at the cart driver now. "We don't want any trouble, Lennox," he said. "All we want are the barrels of salt beef. Just get down and let us have them."

The cart driver didn't move for a long moment. Caroline held her breath. Uncle Aaron was so still that she thought he might be holding his breath, too.

Finally the driver climbed slowly to the ground. It looked as if he muttered something, but Caroline couldn't hear what he said. The lead robber got into the cart, settled himself on the seat, and picked up the lines. "Get up!" he called to the horse hitched to the cart. One wheel screeched in protest as he turned the cart around.

The cart lurched away with the other thieves walking beside it. The original driver stood in the

road, watching as the cart disappeared around
a bend.

Uncle Aaron called, "The danger has passed,
girls."

The girls stood and slid back onto the wagon seat.
"Papa, when I heard that musket, I thought someone
had shot at you!" Lydia's voice trembled.

Uncle Aaron kissed his daughter and squeezed
Caroline's shoulder reassuringly. "I hoped to con-
vince those men to leave quietly. It wasn't a good
idea, though. Not with you girls in the wagon."

"Not *ever*!" Lydia protested.

Caroline agreed. She was proud of Uncle Aaron
for trying to stop the robbery, but she didn't want
him to take such a chance again.

The man who'd been robbed kicked angrily at
a stone. Then he trudged to the wagon. He was a
lean man of medium height, with dark hair streaked
with gray. Beneath his hat, his eyes had narrowed
with frustration, and his face was set in angry lines.

"I appreciate what you tried to do," he said to Uncle Aaron. "Thank you."

Uncle Aaron introduced himself and the girls. "Are you all right?" he asked.

"Furious, but unharmed." The man sighed. "I'm Sidney Lennox, customs officer for this area. I'm in charge of making sure Americans don't sell food or supplies to the British, or buy British goods."

"It seems that illegal trading does indeed take place," Uncle Aaron observed.

"Smugglers are doing a brisk business," Mr. Lennox agreed grimly. "I have only a few deputies to help me."

"Were the men who stole your cart smugglers?" Lydia asked.

Mr. Lennox nodded. "A week ago I found a rowboat hidden in some cattails along the shore of Lake Ontario and started keeping watch. Last night I saw a man drive up right at dusk and load several barrels into the rowboat. I believe he meant to deliver those barrels to a British ship anchored somewhere just offshore."

"Gracious!" Caroline exclaimed. It was spooky to imagine British ships sneaking so close to the American shore.

Mr. Lennox continued, "I tried to arrest the man, but he dove into the water and swam away. My most important task was to keep those barrels from reaching our enemy, so I didn't give chase. I transferred the barrels of salt beef from the rowboat to my own cart. I camped out nearby, and this morning I set out for Sackets Harbor. As you saw, however, the farmer wanted his meat back. He and his friends came after me."

"I've heard that the smuggling problem is getting worse around here," Uncle Aaron said. "You work from Sackets Harbor?"

"I do." Mr. Lennox pulled his hat off and ran a hand through his hair. "It's not the first time I've been forced at gunpoint to give goods back to smugglers."

Caroline glared toward the road where the smugglers had disappeared. "And they stole your horse and cart, too!"

"I'll likely get them back," Mr. Lennox said. "Most of the smugglers have a certain sense of honor. They're willing to sell food to the British, but they wouldn't dream of stealing a man's horse. I expect that they'll leave my horse and cart somewhere where I can find them. There's an abandoned farm some miles west of here—that's where I found them last time."

"You're welcome to ride with us," Uncle Aaron told Mr. Lennox. "I'm only going a mile or so farther, though. I borrowed the horse and wagon from neighbors, and I need to return them."

"That's kind of you," Mr. Lennox said. "I'll go as far as your place and walk from there." He climbed into the wagon bed.

As they continued their journey, Caroline thought through what had happened. It seemed strange that men who sold food illegally to the British would take time to return Mr. Lennox's horse and cart! Perhaps they were desperate farmers like the ones Uncle Aaron had mentioned, men who became smugglers simply to survive. Should she be at least a little sympathetic?

No, she decided, folding her arms across her chest. All smugglers were traitors. Nothing made up for that. *Nothing.*

The afternoon was growing late by the time Uncle Aaron drove into the yard. The farm wasn't much to look at—just a small cabin, a fenced garden, an old cowshed, and a little field where Uncle Aaron was struggling to clear trees and raise crops. Still, Caroline knew that her cousin, aunt, and uncle had worked very hard here.

She expected to find the farm silent and still. Instead, a plume of smoke was drifting from the cabin chimney. "Uncle Aaron?" she asked uneasily.

The front door flew open—and Aunt Martha stepped outside. "There you are!" she called, waving happily.

"Mama!" Lydia jumped from the wagon and ran to her mother. Uncle Aaron was close on her heels.

Caroline climbed to the ground more slowly. Lydia had said that Aunt Martha was still away. What was she doing at the farm?

Aunt Martha caught Caroline's gaze and hurried to the wagon. "I didn't know I'd have the extra pleasure of seeing you, my dear!" She folded Caroline into a warm hug.

"Papa and I asked Caroline to come back and help us," Lydia explained. "We didn't think you'd be home any time soon."

"It's kind of you to come, Caroline." Aunt Martha's smile faded. "And I'm afraid I'm not home for long. Just one night."

Lydia's face fell. "Oh, *Mama*—"

"My sister is still very sick," Aunt Martha explained soberly. "And her children are much younger than you. I'm needed there."

"Of course," Lydia said. Her shoulders slumped, but she nodded.

"But I've missed you terribly," Aunt Martha added. "When I heard that a friend planned to travel in this direction, I decided to come home for a quick visit." She turned to Mr. Lennox, who'd been standing by the wagon with his hat in hand. "Good day to you, sir! I don't believe we've met."

Mr. Lennox introduced himself. "I'm glad to meet you, ma'am. I'll be on my way now. I hope to catch up with my horse and cart."

Aunt Martha flapped a hand as if Mr. Lennox had said something silly. "Surely you can spare time for supper! I've cooked a lovely stew, and we'd be honored to share it."

"That's kind, ma'am," Mr. Lennox said. "I'm happy to accept."

Aunt Martha turned toward the cabin, still chatting with the customs officer. Lydia stayed close, and Caroline started to follow.

Then she noticed Uncle Aaron. He was still standing in the yard, staring off toward the small cowshed, or perhaps the woods beyond that. Worry lined his face. He closed his eyes and rubbed his forehead.

"Uncle Aaron? Is everything all right?" Caroline asked.

Uncle Aaron looked startled, as if he hadn't realized that she was still nearby. "I was just thinking that I've come to love this place," he said softly. "It was hard to leave our good farm in Upper Canada when the war started. I never expected I'd need to start over again. But this ragged little farm . . ."

"It's your home now," Caroline said. Home was special. Home was *home*.

"It is indeed." Uncle Aaron kissed the top of her head. "Go on inside and help your aunt. I'll take

Snowflake back to the Sinclairs' place after supper, but for now, I need to stable her."

"Of course," Caroline said quietly. She pulled her valise from the wagon and walked to the cabin. But before slipping inside, she glanced over her shoulder. Her uncle hadn't moved.

Caroline nibbled her lower lip fretfully. Aunt Martha's surprise visit should have been enough to make Uncle Aaron forget his worries about the farm, as least for the moment. But he seemed more troubled than ever.

chapter 3

An Argument

AUNT MARTHA HAD cooked carrots, potatoes, and peas from the garden, flavored with herbs and a few of the wild leeks that had given Caroline such trouble. When everyone gathered around the table, Caroline discovered that the "lovely stew" Aunt Martha had promised was more of a soup, watered down to feed five. But her aunt had brought a sack of wheat flour home and had baked bread. Lydia proudly produced a plate of butter to go with it.

Aunt Martha asked eagerly about everything that had happened at the farm while she'd been away, but finally she looked at Mr. Lennox. "Please forgive us. We haven't been courteous to a guest. Tell us, how are you faring in your work? Are you catching many smugglers?"

Mr. Lennox shook his head. "Not enough. When I do seize smuggled goods, I'm often overpowered by the smuggler and his friends, as I was today, and am forced to give them back."

"Can't the army help you?" Aunt Martha asked.

"These days the army officers need all their men to fight." Mr. Lennox spread butter on a piece of bread. "But the soldiers in Sackets Harbor have been told to watch for anyone driving cattle through the village. The British pay more for fresh beef than salted meat, so farmers sometimes try to drive their animals east, where it's easier to cross into Upper Canada."

Caroline nodded. Here, a huge lake stretched between Upper Canada and New York. East of Sackets Harbor, only the Saint Lawrence River marked the boundary.

"For now, my men are the only ones patrolling the roads and watching Lake Ontario's shoreline," Mr. Lennox continued. "I hope to get some soldiers assigned to help us when cold weather settles in, though. Smuggling gets worse in the winter."

"Why is that, sir?" Caroline asked.

He explained, "Once Lake Ontario freezes over, anyone in these parts can drive a sleigh right across the ice to British territory."

Lydia sighed. "It's shameful that Americans sell food to our enemy."

"It's not only food," Mr. Lennox told her. "Smugglers can earn the most money by selling ashes."

"Ashes!" Caroline exclaimed. "Why do the British want ashes?"

Mr. Lennox scraped the last bit of soup from his bowl. "Have you ever made lye?" he asked.

"Of course!" she said promptly. "I've helped make lye soap many times." Grandmother saved ashes in a barrel, and at soap-making time, Caroline helped pour water through the barrel. The liquid that came out through a hole in the bottom of the barrel was lye. The lye was cooked with lard to make a creamy soap that hardened as it aged.

"Well, lye has many uses," Mr. Lennox said. "If that lye is boiled and boiled, all the liquid will eventually cook away. What's left in the kettle is called potash. Cloth factories in England use potash to clean wool and bleach cotton."

"Potash isn't used just for cloth, though," Aunt Martha said quietly. "Isn't that right, Mr. Lennox?"

"Potash is used to produce many things," Mr. Lennox agreed. "Including gunpowder."

"Gunpowder?" Caroline gasped. She had lived through two attacks on Sackets Harbor. As bad as it was to know that New York food was feeding enemy sailors and soldiers, it was even worse to discover that Americans were selling the British an ingredient for gunpowder.

"I hope you arrest every smuggler in New York," Lydia said fiercely.

"I'd like to," Mr. Lennox said. "But I have to identify them first."

"How can we help?" Caroline asked impulsively. This conversation was making her feel steamy inside.

Mr. Lennox looked startled. "I know you mean well, Miss Caroline, but smuggling is serious business. Leave it to the adults."

Caroline's face grew hot. She felt embarrassed... but she also felt confused. Her parents and grandmother had taught her to look for ways to help solve problems.

"Your heart is in the right place, Caroline," Uncle Aaron said with an understanding smile. Then he turned to his wife. "Martha, I do need to return Snowflake to the Sinclairs yet tonight. I'll fill the wood box and fetch in water before I go."

"I'll give you a hand," Mr. Lennox offered.

Once those chores were done, the men came back inside so that Mr. Lennox could say good-bye. "Mrs. Livingston, thank you for the fine meal."

"Are you sure you don't wish to spend the night?" Aunt Martha asked.

He shook his head. "As I explained to your husband earlier, I know where my horse and cart might be. If I leave now, I can get there before dark." He and Uncle Aaron left the cabin together.

Aunt Martha surveyed the table. "If you girls wash the dishes, I'll go do the milking." She followed the men outside.

Caroline and Lydia filled a kettle with cold water and hung it over the fire. "This will take a while to heat," Lydia said. "Why don't we go visit the cows, too? Wait till you see how much Garnet has grown!"

When the girls left the cabin, Caroline was surprised to see the wagon still sitting near the cowshed. "I thought your father was headed straight to the Sinclair place."

Lydia shrugged. "He must have seen some chore that needed tending."

As they walked to the shed, Caroline looked around the little farm. Uncle Aaron was slowly clearing land. He killed trees by hacking a ring of bark away from their trunks. Daylight was fading, and the dead trees gave the place a spooky, forlorn look.

"See our brush pile?" Lydia said. She pointed at an enormous pile of branches and logs. "Papa's done most of the work, but I've helped a bit by dragging branches to the pile. That's what the men will help us burn in a few days."

The brush pile was taller than Caroline! For the first time, she realized just how many barrels of ashes a farmer could produce. She remembered all the fires they'd passed on their journey that day. Even now, the air held a faint tang of wood smoke. Farm families used ashes to make soap, and to discourage caterpillars from eating cabbage plants, and to make icy walkways less slippery. They had no use for huge quantities, though. *It must be very tempting for struggling farmers to earn a bit of money by making and selling potash*, she thought.

The idea was discouraging, and Caroline pushed it from her mind. She could hardly wait to see the cows again, and Garnet was good at making them laugh. Now that the sun was setting, the day's heat had eased. A nearby bird began trilling its lovely song: *Whip-poor-will! Whip-poor-will!*

As the girls approached the cowshed, Lydia suddenly held up one hand. "Listen," she whispered.

Caroline heard it too—the sound of hushed voices, coming from the cowshed. The conversation held a sharp edge of anger. Lydia crept closer to the shed, and Caroline followed.

". . . a decision like that without talking to me?" Aunt Martha was saying.

"It was my decision to make," Uncle Aaron muttered.

"No, Aaron. You *must* not do this."

"I have no choice! I've considered what vegetables we have in the garden, and figured how much food we'll need to get Minerva and Garnet through the winter. We simply don't have enough to survive until spring. And I've got to make another land payment in September."

Lydia looked at Caroline with alarm. Caroline could tell that her cousin hadn't realized how bad her family's situation truly was. *I didn't realize either*, she thought uneasily.

Aunt Martha was saying, "There has to be another way."

"There is no other way!" Uncle Aaron exploded. "Do you think I haven't lain awake, night after night, trying to figure out how to make ends meet? With a good ox, I could haul timber to the sawmill and sell it, but there isn't an ox to be had at any price. I can't ask Mr. Sinclair to loan me his team day after day. The *only* thing I can do is—"

"No!" Aunt Martha cried. "It's too dangerous, Aaron. The risk is too great. *Please* don't . . ."

Lydia whirled and quickly walked away.

Caroline followed her cousin back to the cabin. As she went inside, Lydia lit a candle in a tin holder. She avoided Caroline's gaze as she took the kettle of water from the fire, placed it on the table, and shaved bits of lye soap into it. Silently, Caroline poured cold water into a basin and began gathering the dirty soup bowls. She felt ashamed for eavesdropping and didn't know what to say.

Finally Lydia said, "I've never heard my parents disagree like that before." She swished her hand to make a few suds in the dishwater. "I knew Papa was worried about money, but I didn't know how bad things were." She scrubbed a bowl with more force than was necessary and handed it to Caroline.

Caroline dipped it in the rinse water and wiped it dry. "I'm sure everything will be all right."

Lydia picked up another bowl. "Oh, Caroline, what do you think Papa has decided to do? What would have made my mother so upset?"

Caroline remembered how fierce Aunt Martha had sounded. *It's too dangerous, Aaron. The risk is too great.* **Please** *don't* . . . Caroline couldn't imagine what Uncle Aaron intended to do.

Lydia stared at her cousin. "Do you think he plans to join the army or the navy?"

"Oh, surely not," Caroline said. "He couldn't do that and keep the farm going too. Maybe we should just ask your parents what they were talking about."

"No!" Lydia looked horrified. "I don't want them to know we were listening."

Before Caroline could answer, Aunt Martha walked through the door. She looked a little flustered, but she put on a bright smile for the girls. "I stored the milk in the springhouse to cool overnight, and Aaron is on his way to the Sinclair place to return Snowflake and the wagon," she said. "Who wants some sassafras tea?"

"I'll heat more water," Lydia offered. When her mother's back was turned, Lydia gave Caroline a stern look that said *Don't say anything about the argument we overheard!* Caroline nodded.

"I was pleased to bring the flour home," Aunt Martha told them, "and I have one more surprise gift from my sister's farm. They raise sheep, and after shearing them last spring, they had more fleeces than they could handle. I brought several home."

"That's good news!" Caroline exclaimed. A fleece was all the wool clipped from one sheep. Once the wool was cleaned and combed, Lydia and Aunt Martha could spin yarn.

Lydia looked pleased. "Now we'll be able to knit socks and mittens this winter."

Aunt Martha chatted with the girls for the rest of the evening, but Caroline thought she seemed distracted. When Uncle Aaron returned from the Sinclair farm, everyone went to bed.

Lydia and Caroline climbed to the loft and put on their nightgowns, but Caroline had trouble sleeping. She thought Lydia was awake too, but her cousin didn't whisper as she usually did. Caroline didn't hear the murmur of conversation from below, or Uncle Aaron's snores. The silence in the cabin felt heavy, full of unspoken worries and unhappiness.

All the day's questions played through Caroline's mind. She remembered Uncle Aaron's frustration when he spoke of not being able to purchase an ox, and the worry in his eyes as he'd stared into the woods before supper. And she remembered how upset Aunt Martha had sounded during the argument: *No! It's too dangerous, Aaron. The risk is too great.* **Please** *don't do this . . .*

In the dark stillness, a troublesome thought wormed into Caroline's mind. She didn't want to believe that Uncle Aaron might be planning to smuggle potash to the British. But what other choice could he have made?

chapter 4

Searching for Clues

THE NEXT MORNING, the friends who'd driven Aunt Martha home returned right after breakfast. Aunt Martha was ready with her valise packed.

"Safe travels, my dear," Uncle Aaron told his wife. The words were right, but Caroline could tell that Aunt Martha and Uncle Aaron were still unhappy about their argument. It hurt Caroline's heart.

"I wish you could stay longer," Lydia said.

"I do as well," Aunt Martha replied. "But since that isn't possible, I'm grateful to have you and Caroline to depend upon while I'm away." She hugged each girl.

"I'll do everything I can to help," Caroline promised.

As the wagon carrying Aunt Martha disappeared, Caroline couldn't help noticing how sad Lydia looked.

"Let's go see the cows," Caroline suggested.

"Yes, let's." Lydia swiped at her eyes.

The girls went to the cowshed and let themselves into the big stall. "Garnet, it's me!" Caroline called to the red calf. Garnet gave her a *Where have you been?* look before ambling over.

Caroline patted the calf fondly. "You *have* gotten big!" she said. Garnet bobbed her head once in agreement. Even Lydia had to laugh at that.

The girls did the milking and let the cows into the pasture before going back to the cabin. Uncle Aaron was lifting his musket from the wall as they came inside. "I'm going hunting," he said. For some reason, he did not meet their eyes. "I'm not sure when I'll be back." He walked out of the cabin.

Lydia stepped to the front window and watched her father disappear into the woods. Her face was clouded with concern again.

Caroline decided that this was the perfect moment to fetch the surprise hidden in her valise. "Please wait

right here," she told Lydia. "And close your eyes."
Caroline climbed to the loft and retrieved the gift.

Back downstairs, she arranged her surprise on
the bed. "No peeking," she warned, smoothing one
last wrinkle away. "All right! You may look now."

Lydia gasped when she opened her eyes. "A quilt!"

"It's just a *top*," Caroline said. "It will take a lot of
work to finish the actual quilt, but it's a gift for you."

"Truly?" Lydia stepped back, surveying the patchwork with wonder. "But... who pieced it?"

"When I returned to Sackets Harbor after my last
visit with you, Rhonda and I decided to make a quilt
for your new home," Caroline explained. Rhonda was
a good friend who boarded with Caroline's family.
"We designed the central block with an eagle to show
our patriotic spirit." She pointed to the eagle.

"You did a fine job," Lydia assured her. "And
I love all the different nine-patch blocks."

Caroline proudly considered the pieced blocks
surrounding the eagle. In each, nine small squares

were sewn together to make a colorful checkerboard pattern. "Rhonda and I wanted to make the whole quilt top by ourselves, but when word came that you needed me here again, I knew we'd never finish in time. So friends and neighbors pitched in." She squeezed Lydia's hand. "Think of this as a gift from *all* of your friends in Sackets Harbor."

"Oh, *thank* you, Caroline." Lydia's eyes were shining. "Sometimes this little cabin feels quite dreary. Now I have something cheerful to look at every single day."

Caroline plopped down onto a bench. "But we do need to turn the top into a quilt."

"How wonderful that Mama brought fleeces home!" Lydia said. "We can use wool for the batting."

"That will be perfect," Caroline agreed. A quilt was like a sandwich. The pieced quilt top was the top slice of bread, and the wool batting would form the middle layer. Having plenty of wool meant that she and Lydia could make a thick, warm batting—perfect for New York's cold winters.

Lydia hugged the colorful quilt top to her chest, as if already taking pleasure in the good wishes stitched into every block. "We'll still need material for the backing."

"Yes." Caroline nodded. The bottom layer of a quilt was usually made from an old sheet, or sometimes from several large pieces of fabric sewn together. "I brought a few pieces of cloth from my workbox, but not enough to make the backing."

"I can ask our neighbors if they have any cloth to spare," Lydia said. "But it will also take a lot of thread to stitch the top, batting, and backing together."

Caroline sighed. It took lots and *lots* of stitching to hold the layers of a quilt together.

"Perhaps we can trade chores for what we need," Lydia suggested.

That idea lifted Caroline's spirits. "If we can find enough thread and cloth, we can hold a quilting bee."

"A quilting bee will be *just* the thing to cheer up

our neighbors," Lydia agreed. "We're not the only people worried about getting through the coming winter."

My surprise was even better than I'd imagined, Caroline thought. It was wonderful to see Lydia looking excited.

After tidying the cabin, Caroline and Lydia went outside to weed the vegetable garden. When Lydia opened the garden gate, Caroline was astonished. "Everything has grown so much since I was last here!" she exclaimed. Peas and cucumbers were ready to pick. Carrots waited to be dug. Cobs of corn on their tall stalks were fat and tasseled.

Lydia wiped sweat from her forehead. "The garden has done well, considering that we got a late start planting it," she agreed. "But . . ." Her voice trailed away.

But it won't provide enough food to last through the winter. Caroline finished the thought in her mind.

Uncle Aaron hadn't come home by the time the sun was high overhead, so the girls ate a meal of bread and cheese without him. "The neighbor men will be here to help burn brush the day after tomorrow," Lydia reminded Caroline. "I'll use the flour Mama brought to bake bread for them. Most folks just have cornmeal, so that will be a treat."

"Good thing I came to help," Caroline said. She was a little nervous about preparing such a big meal, and she could tell that Lydia was too. "Let's figure out exactly what we need to do."

As the girls planned the meal they would serve the work crew, Caroline noticed Lydia looking out the window frequently. It did seem strange that Uncle Aaron's hunting expedition had kept him away for so long. He usually didn't have any trouble finding game.

Finally Lydia turned her back to the window. "Why don't we go visiting this afternoon?" she asked. "We can tell Mrs. Sinclair about the quilt project."

"That's a fine idea," Caroline declared.

"Tuck a handkerchief into your pocket," Lydia reminded her. "We may pass more smoky burn piles today."

Caroline climbed to the loft and dug through her valise. She had no trouble finding her handkerchief, but... "Oh, feathers!" she said, frustrated.

"What's wrong?" Lydia called.

Caroline came back down. "I forgot to bring a pocket. I do wish that pockets were just sewn into our skirts! That would be so much nicer." She had two pockets at home that she'd stitched of cotton and decorated with embroidery. She usually tied one around her waist so that it hung over her petticoat, hidden under her skirt. A little slit in the seam of her skirt let her reach into the pocket.

Lydia held out her hand. "I'll carry your handkerchief for you." She tucked Caroline's away with her own.

The girls walked along the rutted road that led through the woods to the Sinclair farm. The afternoon was sticky-hot, and sweat trickled down Caroline's backbone. Leaves hung limply from their branches. The faint smell of smoke slipped ghostlike among the trees, reminding her of everything Mr. Lennox had said about potash.

"I can't smell smoke without wondering if one of our neighbors is making potash to sell to the British," Lydia admitted, as if she understood Caroline's thoughts.

Heat and worries made Caroline feel a bit cross. "I wish there was a way we could help Mr. Lennox." She thought for a moment. "We should keep our eyes and ears open. Sometimes people say things around children that they would never say in front of other adults."

"That's true," Lydia allowed. "If we see or hear anything suspicious, we'll tell Papa so that he can pass it on to Mr. Lennox."

Having a plan made Caroline feel better. "We'll start while we're visiting the Sinclairs."

"I can't imagine that the Sinclairs are smugglers," Lydia protested. "They're so nice!"

Caroline shook her head. "We must consider everyone. If we don't, we might miss a clue."

"I suppose you're right," Lydia said reluctantly. She was quiet for a moment. Then she said, "Caroline, you don't think my papa is planning to smuggle potash, do you?"

"*No.*" Caroline was ashamed to admit that the thought had indeed entered her mind.

"He wouldn't." Lydia sounded relieved, as if she'd been afraid of Caroline's answer. "His plan must be about something else."

"It must," Caroline agreed. But what other plan would have frightened Aunt Martha so? Caroline wished Uncle Aaron would explain what he was up to. Without knowing, there was nothing to do but worry.

chapter 5
A Terrible Loss

WHEN THE GIRLS reached the Sinclair farm, Caroline could tell with one glance that the elderly couple had been settled there for at least a few years. An extra room had been added to their log cabin, the field near the house was cleared of trees and stumps, and the animal barn was much larger than Uncle Aaron's. The garden was quite large also, and cheerful flowers had been planted among the vegetables. Caroline saw a pillar of black smoke in the distance, suggesting that Mr. Sinclair was clearing a new field.

Mrs. Sinclair's kind eyes twinkled happily when she saw her guests in the doorway. She had pinned a checked apron over her dress, and she wore a tidy white cap over her gray hair. "Why, if it isn't Lydia and Caroline, come to call! Come in, girls." She beckoned them inside.

Caroline inhaled deeply. "It smells wonderful in here!"

"Wild plums are just coming ripe." Mrs. Sinclair pointed to a pot simmering over a low fire in the hearth. "I'm making jam. Would you like a taste?"

Soon they were all seated at the table, enjoying biscuits spread with steaming jam. "I'm delighted to see you," Mrs. Sinclair told them. "I'm always glad of company, especially when my husband is away from the cabin. He took the oxen out to work a new field. I feel lonely when I don't see him all day."

"Well, we have some fun news," Lydia said. "We hope to have a quilting bee." She told Mrs. Sinclair about the quilt top that needed to be finished.

Mrs. Sinclair's face lit with pleasure. "A party! It would be lovely to get all the ladies together to sew and visit."

Caroline licked a blob of jam from her finger.

"We can't schedule the quilting bee unless we can find enough material to make the quilt backing," she cautioned, "and thread for all the stitching. We hope to trade chores for them."

"I can make all the thread you need." Mrs. Sinclair waved a hand as if to say, *It's no problem at all.*

Lydia's eyebrows rose with surprise. "Really?"

"I've been raising flax for several years. No one else in this area has any, but I brought seeds along when Mr. Sinclair and I moved here. Did you notice the pretty blue flowers outside? Those are flax plants."

"Linen comes from flax plants, right?" Caroline asked. She was familiar with linen cloth, which was tough and long lasting.

"That's right," Mrs. Sinclair said. "There are fibers inside the stems that I spin into linen thread. I have just a little thread at the moment, but if you'll help prepare some flax fibers, I can spin more."

Caroline and Lydia exchanged an eager glance. "We're happy to help," Lydia said.

"Let's go out to the barn, then," Mrs. Sinclair said. "I'll show you my tools for cleaning flax."

The log barn was similar to the cowshed on Lydia's farm, but much larger. With only one window cut into a wall, the space was dim. Some tools hung from pegs on the walls. A shovel and a rake were propped in one corner. Two animal stalls were empty. Snowflake stood in the last stall. The big room smelled musty.

Caroline reminded herself to look for any signs of smuggling. But the first thing she noticed made her feel homesick instead of curious. "Oh—my parents keep ledgers that look just like that," she exclaimed, pointing to a leather-bound book propped on a beam.

"My husband carefully records every bushel of grain he harvests," Mrs. Sinclair said soberly. "Every load of hay, every basket of peas."

Caroline nodded. Evidently Uncle Aaron wasn't the only person keeping close track of food. She hated to think that sweet Mrs. Sinclair might not have enough to eat this winter.

Still... might that worry be enough to make smuggling tempting for the Sinclairs? Caroline studied the barn. She didn't see anything unusual—no boxes or barrels that might hold potash or salt beef. She wasn't sure what to think about a couple of long, skinny bags that had been tossed over a peg on the wall. They looked like they'd been made from old blankets. The shape was unusual—might they be used to carry potash? She stepped closer and put her hand against one of the bags. It was flat and empty, and it felt damp. Caroline couldn't imagine that a smuggler would carry potash in wool, which provided little protection from rain. A wooden keg or leather bag would make a much better container.

Whatever the bags were used for, the Sinclairs obviously didn't let even a worn-out blanket go to waste. Caroline also noticed signs that the Sinclairs had more chores than they could manage. Soiled straw was piled in a corner. The wooden pitchfork leaning against Snowflake's stall had a broken prong. This farm might be larger than Lydia's, but the Sinclairs seemed to be no better off than Caroline's relatives.

Snowflake nickered and stamped one foot. "We should have brought a carrot for her!" Lydia said.

"I used to bring carrots for Bess," Mrs. Sinclair said. "She was such a sweet creature—more like a friend than a horse. I'm afraid Snowflake would nip if one of us tried to feed her."

It's a shame Mr. Sinclair needed to trade Bess for Snowflake, Caroline thought. It sounded as if Mrs. Sinclair needed all the friends she could find.

"Well," Mrs. Sinclair said briskly. "Here are last year's flax plants." She showed the girls a pile of dry, brittle stalks piled in one corner. If stood on end, they'd come about to Caroline's waist.

"It's hard to believe that you can make thread from these!" Lydia marveled.

Mrs. Sinclair showed them the special wooden tool, called a flax break, used to pound the stalks. Pounding the stalks crumbled their hard outer shells into tiny pieces. "The job is too much for me these days," she said. "But with your help, I'll have plenty of fibers to spin into thread for your quilt."

Caroline and Lydia took turns energetically pounding flax stalks with the wooden break. Caroline liked having a good reason to make noise. It was satisfying to think about smuggling and land payments while she crushed the flax stalks. Bam! Bam! *Bam!*

The hard stalks gradually turned into limp, tangled masses. "See the long fibers inside?" Mrs. Sinclair held up a handful of the pounded stalks.

Caroline leaned closer. "I do!"

Mrs. Sinclair scraped away most of the hard bits of stalk and then pulled the fibers through a special comb made with sharp iron teeth. When she was finished, she had a handful of long, clean fibers.

"These are the fibers I will spin into thread on my spinning wheel," she said.

"That clump looks like a horse's tail!" Lydia observed.

Mrs. Sinclair pulled a handful of waste bits from the comb and tossed them into a barrel.

"And that looks like tangled hair left behind in a comb," Caroline added.

"Oh, I've got baskets of that stuff," Mrs. Sinclair said. "I can spin it into heavy twine if I need to, but I much prefer to make fine thread with the nice long fibers." She smiled. "And thanks to your good work, I'll be able to spin thread for your quilting bee."

Caroline grinned. "Now we just need to find enough cloth to make the quilt backing."

As they walked back to the cabin, Mrs. Sinclair asked, "Have you talked with Flora Pemberton? She's an excellent seamstress, and she might have fabric to spare."

Lydia looked at Caroline. "Flora lives at Pemberton

Cove, by Lake Ontario. If Papa doesn't mind, we could visit her tomorrow."

"Ooh, let's!" Caroline said, bouncing on her toes. It would be lovely to get even a quick glimpse of the lake. "Are we really close enough to visit?"

"It's a long walk," Lydia warned.

"I don't mind at all," Caroline declared.

The three went back into the cabin. "Drink some water before you walk home," Mrs. Sinclair advised. "This heat is dreadful."

Caroline tried to think of a polite way to get Mrs. Sinclair talking about smuggling. "Do you know Mr. Lennox, ma'am?" she asked. "He's the local customs officer. We saw some smugglers take his horse and cart yesterday, and I've been hoping they were returned."

Mrs. Sinclair filled two cups from a clay pitcher. "I'm afraid I don't know about the horse and cart, but ... *oh!*" She shook her head. "The smuggling problem is a *disgrace*. Mr. Sinclair and I moved here from back east, along the Saint Lawrence River, and the problem was even worse there. What kind of person would profit by selling goods to the enemy during a war?"

Mrs. Sinclair looked so upset that Caroline was sorry she'd spoken. But before she could respond, she heard a frantic shout from outside.

"That's my husband!" Mrs. Sinclair jumped to her feet in alarm.

Mr. Sinclair burst through the open door, gasping for breath. He'd lost his hat, his cheeks were scratched, and his shirt was dark with sweat.

"Are you unwell?" Mrs. Sinclair asked sharply. "Is it your heart?"

"My heart—is fine," he managed. "But the oxen— they're gone!"

"*What?*" Caroline gasped.

Mr. Sinclair dropped onto a bench. "I eat my noon meal in the field so I don't waste daylight coming back to the cabin," he explained to Caroline and

Lydia. "I always unyoke the team. They often wander into the woods, but they never go farther than the creek nearby. Today, though, they were nowhere to be found."

"How could such great creatures disappear so quickly?" Lydia looked confused.

"I did doze off at noontime," Mr. Sinclair admitted. "I'm not sure how long I was asleep."

Caroline had often watched the workers at Abbott's Shipyard using oxen to haul timber from the woods. Although oxen had minds of their own, she knew that they weren't inclined to roam far. "Would you like us to help you look for them?" she offered.

Mr. Sinclair shook his head mournfully. "It's no use. I've been searching for the last hour or so, with no luck."

"Perhaps they'll come home on their own," Mrs. Sinclair said. The words were brave, but her voice trembled.

"Perhaps," Mr. Sinclair echoed, although the

weary way he rubbed his forehead told Caroline that he was doubtful. "Before the war, I knew that anyone who found my team would bring them back. But now . . . well, we all know the British are paying a high price for beef. I fear the worst."

Caroline and Lydia shared a dismayed glance. "You've always been kind about loaning your oxen to men who don't own a team of their own," Lydia said. "Losing the oxen would hurt everyone around here! Surely no one would steal them."

"I hope you're right," Mr. Sinclair said.

Caroline's heart grew heavy. *Losing the oxen would likely ruin the Sinclairs,* she thought. *And Lydia is right— it might ruin some other farmers too.* But if smugglers had somehow gotten their hands on the team of oxen, they were probably gone for good.

chapter 6
An Unexpected Discovery

MRS. SINCLAIR BROKE the troubled silence. "Why don't you go tell our neighbors that the team is missing? It might help." Caroline admired how the elderly woman tried to be encouraging, instead of fretting.

"That's a good idea." Mr. Sinclair stood. "I'll saddle Snowflake and ride out at once."

Caroline, Lydia, and Mrs. Sinclair went outside, and a few minutes later watched Mr. Sinclair lead the pretty white horse from the barn. When Mr. Sinclair swung into the saddle, Snowflake danced sideways.

"Oh, I wish my husband hadn't sold Bess," Mrs. Sinclair murmured. "He has enough troubles without trying to ride a mare that spooks at her own shadow!"

Mr. Sinclair spoke soothingly to Snowflake, and she settled down. "I'll be back when I can," Mr. Sinclair called. Then he rode out of the clearing.

"Pardon me, ma'am," Caroline said, "but has Mr. Sinclair been unwell? You sounded worried earlier."

"He's had a few bad spells," Mrs. Sinclair explained. "He shouldn't work so hard, but it's impossible to slow the man down. Sometimes he does farmwork all day and then goes out after dark to hunt by moonlight." She sighed. "He's not feeble. I just worry because I never know when his heart will give him trouble."

Lydia glanced at the sun, judging how much daylight remained. "Would you like us to stay with you until Mr. Sinclair returns?" she asked.

Mrs. Sinclair tried to smile. "I'll be fine. Let me get you some thread." She fetched a smooth stick with some linen thread wound around it to keep it from tangling. "If you find pieces of cloth for the quilt backing, this should be enough to sew them together. And here—I'll lend you this basket in case you spot plums on your way home."

"We'll let you know when the quilting bee will take place," Caroline promised.

They waved good-bye to Mrs. Sinclair and walked away from the cabin. Two hens scratching for insects in the grass scurried away from the girls. Caroline spotted the blue flax flowers growing in a thick line in the garden. She hoped the cheerful blossoms would lift Mrs. Sinclair's spirits.

Lydia paused to put on her sunbonnet and tie the strings. "Let's go home through the woods instead of taking the road," she suggested. "Who knows? We just might spot the oxen."

"Oh, I hope we do," Caroline said. The Sinclairs seemed like good people and good neighbors. Losing the oxen was a cruel blow.

Lydia led the way around a wheat field, past a field where Mr. Sinclair had been burning brush, and down a narrow footpath to the creek. "This runs through our land," Lydia said. "We can follow it back."

The girls edged their way through the shrubs bordering the creek. Caroline's mood improved when she spotted a thicket dotted with reddish-purple fruit. "Plums!"

"The ripe ones will easily separate from the branches," Lydia said. "Just be careful of thorns."

Before long, they'd filled the basket with fruit. "I'll save most of them for the men's work party at our farm the day after tomorrow," Lydia decided. "We can make a small cobbler just for us tonight, though."

"Maybe that will cheer up your father," Caroline said hopefully.

They continued along the creek until they came to a huge boulder covered with green moss. "This is where we leave the creek," Lydia explained. "If we head straight up the hill, we'll end up at home."

As she followed Lydia up the slope, Caroline

watched her feet so that she wouldn't slip. Away from the burbling creek, the woods felt still. The birds were silent. *I'll never get used to living inland,* she thought. Lake Ontario was never still. Even in winter, winds and deep currents often cracked and heaved the ice.

Suddenly Lydia stopped walking. "Where did *that* come from?"

Caroline almost bumped into her cousin, and she put one hand against a tree to steady herself. "Where did what come from?"

"I'm not sure." Frowning, Lydia pushed a branch aside and slipped around a thick shrub.

When Caroline followed, she saw that someone had hacked down saplings to create a small clearing. A dirty sheet of canvas covered something lumpy in the middle of the open area.

Lydia gestured toward the canvas. "That wasn't here when I gathered fiddlehead ferns last spring. I can't imagine what's under there."

"There's only one way to find out." Caroline marched to the mound. She grabbed one edge of the canvas and threw it aside, revealing an iron kettle hanging from a tripod made from three stout branches. A few charred sticks remained in a fire pit beneath the kettle.

Beside the tripod sat a hollowed-out log, held off the ground by rocks. The trough was filled with ashes. A hole had been drilled at the bottom of the trough, and a clear liquid was dripping into a crock.

"Oh, *no*." Caroline's backbone tingled as she stared at the crock. Lye was made by pouring water through ashes. *If lye is boiled and boiled, all the liquid will eventually cook away,* Mr. Lennox had explained. *What's left in the kettle is called potash.* And the British in Upper Canada paid high prices for potash.

"Somebody has been making potash to smuggle to the enemy," Lydia said grimly.

"And they set up this rig out here in the woods

so that no one would see them doing it," Caroline added. She surveyed the woods around the clearing. "We're still downhill from your farm. Unless they built a huge fire, the smoke probably wouldn't be seen from your place."

"Someone chose this spot *very* carefully," Lydia agreed. "It's also hidden from the creek, and from all the hunting trails I know of."

Caroline peered inside the iron kettle. "I don't see any of those grains of potash Mr. Lennox described. The smuggler must have scraped them out. I suppose carrying them would be no more trouble than carrying a sack of salt."

"Oh, *Caroline.*" Lydia looked miserable. "This is *our* land. Do you think Papa . . ." She couldn't finish the sentence.

Caroline knew what Lydia was thinking. "Well, it's possible that Uncle Aaron didn't really go hunting this morning," Caroline admitted. "Maybe he came here. Maybe this is what he argued with your mother about." She paused, seeing how that idea felt. It didn't feel good.

Lydia straightened her shoulders and shook her head. "*No.* When the war began, my father said he simply could not live in enemy territory. Our family left everything behind in Upper Canada. Now my brother is serving with the American navy. My papa would never do anything to help the British."

Although Caroline wanted desperately to believe that, she couldn't quite shove away a tiny niggle of doubt. *I mustn't let Lydia see my suspicion, though*, she thought. Lydia had enough to worry about without knowing that her cousin wasn't sure of her father's innocence.

Instead, Caroline crouched and stretched her hand over the fire pit. "This spot *is* well hidden, but that just means that anyone might have set up their potash rig here. These embers are barely warm. Somebody was here earlier today, but it's been a while."

"If the smuggler let his fire go out, he's probably finished for the day," Lydia said.

Caroline rose and slowly walked around the clearing, searching for anything that might identify the smuggler. She did discover a pile of firewood almost hidden behind a thicket. The wood had been neatly arranged by size: logs split with an ax into handy chunks to provide the main fuel, smaller sticks for kindling, a pile of twigs and scraps of twine for tinder to get the fire started.

"The smuggler is definitely planning to make more potash here," she told Lydia. "It took work to chop this much wood."

Lydia nodded. "If he's been coming here a lot, maybe he's worn a path through the woods. Maybe we can see what direction he's been coming from."

The girls circled the clearing slowly, searching for any sign of a path through the underbrush. "It's no use," Lydia said finally. "It looks like the smuggler's been careful to come and go from different directions each time."

"I don't think he left behind any clues," Caroline agreed.

"Then let's *go*," Lydia said. "I want to be away from here."

Caroline replaced the canvas covering. As they hurried on up the slope, Caroline asked, "Which of your neighbors can easily reach that potash rig?"

Lydia shifted the heavy basket of plums from one hand to the other. "Well, the Sinclairs are our closest neighbors to the west. The Zahn farm is just as close to the east. Mr. and Mrs. Zahn were born in Germany, but they bought their farm before we came here."

"So either Mr. Sinclair or Mr. Zahn could easily follow the creek and then walk up to that clearing on your land," Caroline said.

"But the Sinclairs are so nice!" Lydia protested. "And the Zahns are too." She sighed. "But I'll tell Papa what we saw, so he can report it to Mr. Lennox. Maybe he can catch the smuggler making potash."

Caroline shook her head. "Mr. Lennox said that he and his deputies are busy watching the roads and patrolling the lakeshore, remember?"

"Well, maybe Papa can spy on the smuggler," Lydia said. "Come along. He's probably home by now."

When Caroline and Lydia reached the cabin, however, there still was no sign of Uncle Aaron. By the time he finally arrived, the girls had a juicy plum cobbler baking.

"I'm glad you're home, Papa!" Lydia exclaimed. "You were gone a long time."

Uncle Aaron pulled two pigeons from the canvas pouch slung over one shoulder. "For dinner."

Uncle Aaron spent the whole day hunting and shot only two pigeons? Caroline thought. Her uncle was a good hunter who usually brought home plenty of meat.

Lydia looked surprised too, but she only asked, "Shall Caroline and I make a pigeon pie for supper? We picked peas and dug carrots this morning."

Uncle Aaron nodded. Then he sat at the table and began to clean his musket.

Lydia asked Caroline a question with her eyes: *Should I tell him about the potash rig we found in the woods?*

Yes! Caroline answered silently. *It's important!*

"Papa," Lydia began hesitantly, "Caroline and I think a smuggler has been—"

Uncle Aaron slammed one fist down on the table. "Not another word about smugglers! I don't want you girls to even *think* about smuggling. Mr. Lennox told you to leave it alone. Besides, a man needs some peace after a long day!"

Lydia's mouth opened. Her cheeks flushed bright red.

Caroline had never heard her kind uncle speak with such impatience. *Perhaps he's still upset after his argument with Aunt Martha*, she thought. She hoped Uncle Aaron would apologize, but he did not.

Finally Caroline grabbed Lydia's hand. "Let's

go dig some baby potatoes," she suggested quietly. "They'll go nicely in the potpie."

By the time they reached the garden gate, tears were spilling down Lydia's cheeks. "You didn't do anything wrong," Caroline whispered.

Lydia swiped her cheeks. "I didn't even have a chance to tell him about the potash rig we found in the woods!"

"We'd better not bother him about it now," Caroline said. "Maybe Mr. Lennox will stop by again, and we can tell him directly."

"Papa probably wouldn't have had time to go down there and spy on the smuggler making potash anyway." Lydia lifted her chin. "Perhaps..."

Caroline could tell they were thinking the same thing, so she finished her cousin's sentence. "Perhaps we need to do some spying ourselves."

It was a good idea, but Caroline's heart felt heavy as a stone. She knew Lydia wanted to prove that someone other than Uncle Aaron had set up the potash rig. *Please, please, **please** let us not find Uncle Aaron making potash,* she thought miserably. If he was involved in smuggling, Caroline didn't think that she—or Lydia—would ever be able to forgive him.

chapter 7

Suspicions

WHEN CAROLINE AND Lydia returned to the cabin, Uncle Aaron did apologize for his outburst. "I'm sorry I lost my temper, girls. I have a lot on my mind, but I should not have gotten cross with you."

"I'm sorry you're so burdened," Lydia said quietly.

Caroline waited for Uncle Aaron to say more— maybe even tell them whatever it was he'd argued about with Aunt Martha. But he grew silent again.

Lydia twisted her fingers together. "Papa? I do need to tell you some bad news." She explained how Mr. Sinclair had lost his oxen.

"That is bad news indeed," Uncle Aaron said. "We must keep a close eye on Minerva and Garnet. We can lock them into the shed at night, and whenever we're all away from home."

Uncle Aaron grew silent again. The girls hauled one of Aunt Martha's fleeces inside and began picking out clumps of dirt and other litter caught in the fibers. Caroline liked working with wool because it felt good in her fingers. But she wished that Uncle Aaron would tell stories or jokes as he used to do. She was glad when bedtime came.

"The neighbor men are gathering at dawn tomorrow to harvest wheat at the Zahn place," Uncle Aaron reminded the girls. "There's no need for you to see me off. I'll just have another dish of that delicious plum cobbler for breakfast." His mouth smiled, but it didn't reach his eyes.

"Caroline and I hope to walk to Pemberton Cove after chores tomorrow," Lydia said. "If we may."

"Of course," Uncle Aaron said. "Whatever you wish."

In the loft, the girls slipped into their nightgowns and settled down. Caroline could tell that her cousin did not want to talk about her father's outburst.

"Since we're going to see Flora Pemberton tomorrow, will we have time to go spy on the potash rig in the morning?" Caroline whispered.

"Yes, if we don't linger too long," Lydia whispered back. "We have to discover who is making potash in the woods before someone else finds the rig and blames Papa! We'll just have to creep close very carefully, so we won't be seen if the smuggler is working there."

Caroline felt better knowing that she and Lydia had a plan that might let them identify a smuggler. *I just hope we don't find Uncle Aaron at work,* she thought again.

Lydia fell asleep quickly. Caroline *wanted* to fall asleep too, but questions swirled in her head. Who was making potash in the woods? Why did Uncle Aaron have so little game to show for a whole day's hunting? What had he argued about with Aunt Martha?

The cabin was so quiet that she heard every faint mouse-scurry and breath of wind sighing through the open window downstairs. She missed the sound of

Uncle Aaron's snores. Was he also too troubled to sleep?

Then she heard the quiet creak of a floorboard as Uncle Aaron got out of bed downstairs. A moment later, the front door eased open with a faint wooden scrape.

Caroline slipped from her pallet just as quietly and made her way down the ladder. *I'll feel foolish if Uncle Aaron has simply gone to the outhouse*, she thought. But after finding that potash rig, she needed to make sure he wasn't creeping down the hill to the secret clearing.

She reached the front window just in time to see her uncle, no more than a dark shadow in the moonlight, crossing the yard with a lantern in hand. He walked to the cowshed and disappeared inside.

Caroline crossed her arms, perplexed. *Perhaps Uncle Aaron just wants to check on Minerva and Garnet*, she thought. Even though he'd put a lock and chain on the shed door, those cows were so valuable that he might feel a need to make sure they were safe.

It seemed, however, that he was inside the shed longer than it would take to make sure that all was well. Perhaps ten minutes passed before he came back outside and walked toward the cabin. Caroline scurried to the ladder and climbed to the loft. She was back on her pallet when she heard Uncle Aaron slip inside. The bed creaked as he lay back down. Sometime later, quiet snores let her know that he had finally drifted off.

But Caroline lay awake much longer. What had Uncle Aaron been doing in the shed in the middle of the night?

The next morning, Lydia and Caroline rose just as dawn came creeping across the clearing. The last scoop of plum cobbler was gone, and Uncle Aaron was too.

Caroline didn't know what to do. *Should I tell Lydia I saw her father creep out to the shed last night?* she wondered. She wasn't used to keeping secrets from her cousin. One look at Lydia's troubled face, however, made her decide to hold her tongue—at least for now.

"Well," Lydia said, "let's go tend the cows."

Caroline nodded. Garnet could usually make them smile.

The girls walked out to the shed in soft morning light. A wren sang from the garden fence. Caroline felt her worries ease, just a bit. She liked this time of day.

It was cooler inside the shed, and the air held the pleasant scent of dried grass. Lydia used a wooden pitchfork to toss some hay into the cows' manger. "It's been so hot and dry, there hasn't been much grass for them," she said.

Garnet, who'd been outside in the pasture, immediately poked her red head around the door. Her expression seemed to say, *Is that for me?*

Caroline couldn't help laughing. "Yes, it's for you," she said. The pretty calf came inside and began to munch.

As Lydia forked some soiled straw outside, Caroline looked around the shed. She didn't see any clue to suggest what her uncle had been doing in here. Nothing was out of place. Caroline felt puzzled. Had she been imagining trouble?

As Lydia carried more straw outside, Caroline noticed several wasps flying through the open door. Mud daubers had built their tube-shaped homes high on the rafters, but since they didn't bother people, Caroline never paid them any mind. Now, she tipped her head back and watched one crawl into its home. *Every creature needs a place to call its own*, she thought.

And this farm, this rough little shed, the rocky fields and garden—this was Lydia and Uncle Aaron's place. Caroline swallowed hard. She remembered the look in Uncle Aaron's eyes when she'd said that this place had become his home. *It has indeed*, he'd said. And she remembered that Uncle Aaron soon had to make a land payment, or lose the farm. He must be feeling desperate. As she watched the mud daubers

up in the rafters, she wondered again why Uncle
Aaron had come out to the shed last night.

Then she noticed something unexpected. It looked
as if a dirty string was dangling from the top of the
support beam that ran overhead. Caroline wrinkled
her forehead. Then she pulled her skirt up above her
knees and put one foot in a gap between two boards
that were part of the stall wall.

Lydia came inside and leaned the pitchfork
against the wall. "Mercy, Caroline! What are you
doing?"

"Climbing on top of this pen," Caroline said.
"Doesn't it look like there's something up on that
beam? I want to see what it is." She managed to get
her feet beneath her and stand. "It's teetery up here!"
She put one hand against the wall for balance and
stretched her other hand high overhead to reach
the beam. The wood felt rough and dusty. When
she wiggled her fingers, though, they hit something
smooth. She tried to grasp whatever she'd found.

Instead, it fell from the beam and thudded onto the floor. Caroline stared down at a leather pouch. Someone had tied the pouch closed with a cord. One dangling end of the cord had caught her eye.

Lydia picked up the pouch. "What on earth is this?"

"I don't know," Caroline said. She scrambled down.

Frowning in confusion, Lydia loosened the knot and tipped the pouch over her palm. Several coins fell into her hand. "Why... who would hide money in our shed?"

Caroline sucked in a long breath. She wished now that she had told Lydia what she'd seen in the moonlight. "I think it belongs to your father. I saw him slip out here to the shed last night."

"This can't be Papa's," Lydia objected. "He keeps his money in the cabin."

Caroline tried to think of a good reason why Uncle Aaron would hide money in the cowshed. She tried to think of a good reason he would tiptoe out of the cabin and slip into the locked shed after dark. *Is this money he earned smuggling?* she thought. *Is that why he didn't want us to see it?* She glanced hesitantly at Lydia.

"My father is not a smuggler!" Lydia said sharply.

"I didn't say he was!" Caroline protested, but her cheeks felt hot. She *was* suspicious.

"It's what you're thinking." Lydia's eyes sparked with anger. "I can tell. You've already decided he's guilty."

"I have *not*!" Caroline insisted. "But... well, I can't help wondering."

The girls glared at each other. The shed was quiet. Even Garnet had stopped munching hay, as if she was upset too.

Caroline's anger fizzled away. "I don't *know* what's going on. All I know for sure is that we have enough to worry about without arguing."

After a moment, Lydia nodded. "Come on," she

said quietly. "Let's get the chores done."

"Yes, let's," Caroline said quickly.

Lydia reached for the milking stool. Then she stopped and looked Caroline square in the eye. "Papa would never smuggle," she said, speaking slowly so that each word seemed to carry weight.

"I know he wouldn't," Caroline said, hoping desperately that he wouldn't prove her wrong.

After breakfast, the girls headed back to the clearing where they'd found the potash rig. They approached with caution, tiptoeing through the underbrush. Caroline held her breath, dodging under low-hanging tree branches, trying hard not to step on sticks that might snap and give them away.

Caroline sniffed the air as they crept close. She smelled the green scent of growing plants, and the dusty scent of dry earth, but no telltale whiff of smoke. Lydia held one finger to her lips as they

reached a screen of leafy branches. Caroline pushed
one branch carefully aside, and both girls peeked at
the clearing. No one was there.

"What now?" Lydia whispered.

Caroline walked into the clearing and took a hard
look around. "We might be able to tell if someone
has been here." When she pushed the canvas covering away and peered beneath the hollow log filled
with ashes, she felt a hitch of unease beneath her ribs.
"Yesterday afternoon lye was dripping from a hole
in the bottom into this crock," she reminded Lydia.
"But someone's been here and plugged the hole with
a wooden peg to keep the crock from overflowing."
She studied the plug, carefully avoiding Lydia's gaze.
*Uncle Aaron could have stopped here yesterday on his way
home from his hunting trip,* she thought.

Lydia glanced nervously over her shoulder. "We'd
better get out of here. The smuggler might be on his
way back here right now to boil that lye into potash."

"I think we should wait for a while," Caroline

countered. "If we hide behind the bushes, one of us can spy on the clearing and the other one can watch for the smuggler coming from behind."

"And what will we do if he spots us?" Lydia asked.

The very notion made Caroline feel quivery inside. "We'd better hide so well that he *can't* spot us," she said stoutly, keeping her voice low. After considering several choices, she pointed to an enormous old oak tree growing beside a shrubby thicket. "How about there?"

"Just hurry!" Lydia hissed, glancing over her shoulder again.

Caroline pulled her skirt up, dropped to her hands and knees, and crawled into the thicket. She brushed a few sticks away and sat on a carpet of dead leaves. Lydia followed. "Why don't you keep an eye on the woods," Caroline whispered, "and I'll watch the clearing."

The forest suddenly seemed full of sounds—the flutter of bird wings, the skitter of squirrels' feet, the whisper of leaves nudged by a breeze. At first, Caroline jumped anxiously at every hint of noise. But as she and Lydia waited . . . and waited . . . and *waited*, her nervous excitement faded. She watched a chipmunk dart back and forth across the clearing. She listened to a woodpecker hammering a dead tree nearby. She dug holes in the cool earth with one finger. She wondered again what Uncle Aaron and Aunt Martha had argued about. And still, there was no sign of the smuggler.

Lydia began squirming. Finally she scooched around to face her cousin. "If we don't leave soon, we won't have time to visit Flora Pemberton."

Caroline nodded. Reluctantly, she stood and dusted off her skirt.

"This is so frustrating!" Lydia scowled. "Whoever works this potash rig lives close enough to stop by. It *must* be one of our neighbors."

"Neighbors . . . of *course*!" Caroline shook her head. "We should have known that no one would come today. All of the neighbor men went to the Zahns' work party, right? The smuggler wouldn't dare spend the morning here because the other men would wonder where he was."

"That must be it," Lydia agreed.

As the girls trudged back toward the farm, Caroline imagined the smuggler working side by side with his neighbors—neighbors who had, perhaps, suffered terribly because of the war. The situation made Caroline feel cross. Had similar thoughts made Uncle Aaron so cross the evening before?

Or had Uncle Aaron gotten cross because he didn't want the girls to search for a smuggler and stumble onto his potash rig?

Lydia and I need to know the truth, Caroline thought. Her heart ached with longing to learn that Uncle Aaron had *not* turned to smuggling in order to save his farm. But if he was guilty of smuggling, they deserved to know that too.

chapter 8
The Deputies

CAROLINE WAS DISAPPOINTED that she and Lydia hadn't been able to discover the smuggler using the potash rig in the woods. *At least we have a nice visit to Pemberton Cove to look forward to*, she thought. With any luck, they'd get the cloth needed to finish Lydia's quilt.

They prepared to leave the farm when the sun was high overhead. Lydia tucked the patchwork quilt top into a basket to show to Flora. "That way we'll know exactly how much cloth we need for the backing," she explained. Caroline left the cabin carrying a basket holding a small crock of butter for Flora and a corked bottle of water.

The girls walked through the woods along the main road for quite some time. Neither found much to say, and Caroline wondered if Lydia was still unhappy with her for thinking that Uncle Aaron might be making potash to sell to the British. *I hate all this trouble!* Caroline thought. She wished she'd never heard of smugglers.

Even beneath the huge trees, the air felt like an oven, and Caroline could hardly wait to reach the lakeshore. When they finally approached a turnoff she asked, "Is this where we start north?"

Lydia nodded. "That lane leads straight to Pemberton Cove. It's the only harbor for miles."

"Mr. Lennox told us he seized those barrels of salt beef when a smuggler tried to row them out to a British ship waiting just offshore," Caroline mused. "Maybe Mr. Pemberton is a smuggler."

"Mr. Pemberton has always been kind to me, and Flora is my friend," Lydia said. "And smugglers might hide a small rowboat anywhere along the lakeshore." She pinched her lips together thoughtfully. "But ... you're right. There is a dock at the cove, and

Mr. Pemberton does have a boat. It would be easy for him to slip out to the lake and meet a British ship."

"We must watch for anything suspicious," Caroline said.

After another half mile of walking, the Pemberton place came into view. "I think they have the biggest house between Sackets Harbor and Buffalo," Lydia said.

Caroline scarcely noticed the house. Beyond the clearing was a little cove that opened into her beloved Lake Ontario. A tightness in her chest eased as she looked at the restless blue-green water rippling into the horizon. After worrying about smugglers and land payments and whether Lydia's family would have enough to eat during the coming winter, seeing the lake was a comfort.

She walked quickly past the house and continued down the lane to the shore. The natural bay would provide a bit of protection from heavy storms. A long dock extended into the harbor. A skiff was tied to it, bobbing slightly as if eager to head out into open water. Caroline was sorely tempted to jump in, cast off, and raise the sail.

"Caroline!" Lydia called, catching up to her cousin. "We really should see if Flora and her father are home before wandering about."

"Of course," Caroline agreed, remembering her manners. "I just had to get a look."

Reluctantly, she turned toward the house. It *was* big—two stories, and made of sawn lumber instead of logs. The Pemberton place was the most settled home Caroline had seen since leaving Sackets Harbor. Marigolds and asters bloomed yellow and purple around the house. A barn stood near the edge of the woods. A split-rail fence ran along the edge of the lawn overlooking the harbor.

As the girls approached the house, the front door opened and a slender young woman came outside. "Good day!" she called, waving. She hurried across the lawn to meet them.

Lydia introduced Caroline to Flora Pemberton. Flora looked to be maybe fifteen years old, and she was dressed like a proper young lady. Her stylish cream-colored dress was beautifully embroidered, and she'd curled her dark hair on top of her head.

Caroline became aware of how grubby she looked and felt after the long, hot walk. "I'm pleased to meet you," she said politely. Her cheeks grew even warmer when she noticed that some garden dirt was still caught beneath her fingernails.

Flora didn't seem to notice. "I'm glad you've come!" she exclaimed. "We live so far from town that I get lonely."

"Do you have any brothers or sisters?" Caroline asked.

"My sisters are older, and all married," Flora explained. "My mother died years ago, so now it's just Papa and me. We used to have guests often, since we're a convenient stop for people traveling by ship." She sighed. "But that was before the war."

A man with gray hair and bushy side-whiskers came outside. "There you are, daughter," he said as he joined them. Flora's father wore tan breeches with a clean white shirt, a cream-colored vest, and a fancy white scarf tied around his neck. The pale leather gloves he carried didn't show a single spot or stain. *It's easy to see that Mr. Pemberton is not a farmer,* Caroline thought.

Flora made the introductions. "Papa, this is Caroline Abbott."

Mr. Pemberton's eyebrows rose in surprise. "Abbott... Is your father the shipbuilder? I used to own a pretty little sloop made at Abbott's Shipyard."

Caroline beamed with pride. "Yes, sir. My father is the best shipbuilder in New York State." She glanced at the empty cove. "Do you still have the sloop?"

"The British stole her, blast them." Mr. Pemberton angrily slapped his gloves against one leg. "I'm a merchant, and after the war began I thought I might still travel safely as long as I stayed close to the American shore. But one day a British ship slipped across the lake and threatened to open fire if I didn't surrender the sloop. I had a hold full of expensive goods, and I lost everything. It almost ruined me financially."

"I'm sorry to hear that," Caroline said with heartfelt sympathy. She would never forget the terrible day the British had stolen a sloop that belonged to her family. She and Lydia had been on board and had watched the British capture Papa and Oliver.

"Well, I must be off to Oswego," Mr. Pemberton said, referring to a town farther west along the lakeshore. "I travel by land these days." He kissed Flora's cheek and nodded politely to Lydia and Caroline before walking to the barn. A few moments later, he drove a small wagon from the barn and turned toward the lane.

After waving farewell to him, Flora turned to her guests. "Shall we go inside?"

Caroline found the Pemberton house to be light and roomy. The downstairs was divided into three rooms—a dining room, a sitting room, and a kitchen along the back, facing away from the lake. The three girls settled in the sitting room. Lydia unfolded the quilt top and draped it over a chair.

"Caroline and her friends made this for me," she explained. "We have wool to make a warm middle layer in the quilt, and Mrs. Sinclair promised us thread. But we don't have cloth to make the backing."

"You're welcome to anything I have," Flora said promptly.

"That's *very* generous," Lydia said.

"Let me go get my scrap bag." Flora hurried upstairs. She returned with a bag full of small bits and several larger pieces of neatly folded cotton.

Lydia fingered a piece of cloth printed with red vines and flowers. "I brought a little butter for you, but I'm afraid we don't have much to trade."

"Don't worry about that," Flora said. "My father brings home cloth almost every time he goes to town, and I often trade scraps with other ladies. I'd be happy to see you put some of these pieces to use."

The three girls had fun considering the choices, holding larger pieces against the quilt, figuring what they needed. Lydia's favorite piece wasn't big enough, so they decided to sew long strips from another fabric around the edges to make the quilt backing.

"I think this will be quite nice," Flora said. "Caroline? Would you like to take some cloth along as well?"

Caroline especially loved a dark blue cotton printed with little white flowers. "I forgot to bring a pocket on this trip," she told Flora, "so if you truly don't mind, I'll take these pieces and stitch a new one. Then I can stop pestering Lydia every time I need my handkerchief."

Lydia and Caroline tucked their treasures into their baskets. "Thank you, Flora," Lydia said. "We'll let you know about the quilting bee."

"Why don't we have the quilting bee here?" Flora

clasped her hands with excitement. "We could even invite the husbands and fathers to join us for a picnic supper."

"That's a fine idea," Caroline said, and Lydia agreed. They decided to hold the bee in three days. "We'll have everything ready by then," Lydia promised, and they all waved good-bye.

As they started home, Caroline said, "With the cloth Flora gave us, you'll soon have a finished quilt."

Lydia gave her basket a happy swing. "I'm so excited!"

Caroline was delighted to see her cousin in such good spirits. "Tonight we'll sew the backing," she said. "And then we—oh!" Her voice broke as two men holding muskets stepped from behind a huge tree.

The shorter man was stocky, with deep-set eyes. "What are you girls doing on this road?" he demanded.

We haven't done anything wrong, Caroline reminded herself, but her mouth didn't seem able to form words.

With his bushy eyebrows lowered into a frown, the man's eyes looked more squinty than ever. "I *said*, where are you going? And what's in your baskets? Hand 'em over. *Now*." He had a high, squeaky voice.

"Don't sound so threatening," the taller man said. "There's no need to frighten young girls."

"That's how little you know," Mr. Squinty-Eyes muttered. "Some smuggler might well be sending illegal goods from the lakeshore in these girls' baskets!"

"We're not carrying illegal goods!" Caroline said angrily. She lifted her chin and held out her basket. The two men quickly discovered that she'd spoken truthfully.

"Where are you lasses going?" the tall man asked.

"We're heading home after visiting the Pembertons, sir," Lydia explained. "My father's name is Aaron Livingston, and our farm is a few miles—"

"Oh, we know where *everyone* lives in these parts," Mr. Squinty said.

It seemed to Caroline that Mr. Squinty liked feeling important. "Are you deputies of Mr. Lennox's, sir?" she asked. "Mr. Lennox and my Uncle Aaron are good friends." That was an exaggeration, but she didn't care. "He shared a meal at our cabin just the other day."

Mr. Squinty scowled, but the other man laughed. "We are indeed deputies," he told the girls. "We're looking for British goods that have been smuggled into New York from Upper Canada."

"Or goods that are packed up for sale to the British." Deputy Squinty pulled a big handkerchief from his pocket and mopped his forehead. Caroline almost felt a little sorry for him. His face was red with heat, and his vest was so tight that it looked as if several buttons might pop free at any moment.

The tall man handed back the girls' baskets. "You can be on your way."

"Thank you," Lydia said.

The girls hurried until they rounded a bend and

left the deputies behind. "Gracious," Lydia said, her high spirits gone. "That was unpleasant."

"Mr. Lennox must have posted them there because he *does* think Pemberton Cove is a good place for smuggling," Caroline said. "Although . . . I don't know that Mr. Pemberton is a good suspect after all. The British stole his ship and merchandise! It's hard to believe that he'd want to do business with them after that."

"Or maybe losing so much forced him to become a smuggler," Lydia countered.

Caroline thought that over. "The Pembertons don't look like they're struggling to survive," she agreed. "Flora and her father weren't dressed for hard work. Their house is beautiful, and Flora said her papa often buys cloth for her. How does a merchant earn money after his sloop is gone?"

"I suppose he hauls goods by wagon now," Lydia said. "But the roads are impossible when it gets muddy, or when the winter snow isn't good for sleighing. That *must* hurt his business, yet he seems to be prospering."

Caroline didn't believe that Mr. Pemberton had built the potash rig she and Lydia had found. The hidden clearing was too far away, and he didn't look like a man used to doing hot labor. Still, for the first time, she felt as if she and Lydia had identified someone who might well be a smuggler.

"Let's look for evidence of smuggling when we come back for the quilting party," Caroline said.

"We'll have to be careful." Lydia sounded worried. "We don't want Mr. Pemberton to catch us snooping around."

"No, we don't," Caroline agreed soberly.

Lydia added, "Even if Mr. Pemberton is smuggling, it might be impossible to find proof."

"I know," Caroline said. "But we have to try."

chapter 9
Fire!

SHADOWS WERE STRETCHING long by the time Caroline and Lydia reached a lane branching off the main road. "That's the turnoff to the Zahn farm," Lydia said. "We can stop and tell Mrs. Zahn about the quilting bee, but we can't stay long. We need to get home and tend the cows."

They followed the turnoff. Soon the trees thinned and Caroline saw a farm. "There's your father!" she exclaimed as they entered the clearing.

Beyond the Zahns' log home, Uncle Aaron and eight or nine men were harvesting golden wheat, each with a curved blade mounted on a long handle. Their hats and shirts were dark with sweat. Several boys and two women raked the cut wheat into bundles.

Caroline had never seen wheat being harvested before. It was almost like watching a dance. The men were swinging their scythes in a steady, graceful manner. Well . . . except for a boy wearing a blue vest, who looked a few years older than Lydia. He made one long swing, then one short swing. While most of the men moved through the field of grain in a line, he fell farther and farther behind.

"Who is that?" Caroline asked. "It looks like someone is just learning how to use a scythe."

"Oh, that's Peter Zahn." Lydia shook her head. "I think he could keep up with the men if he wanted to. I heard Papa say that Peter doesn't like to work hard."

As the men reached the field's edge, Caroline could hear *phisht-phisht-phisht* sounds as the blades cut through the stalks. When the men finished their row, they paused to drink from jugs left under a tree. Uncle Aaron grinned when he noticed Lydia and Caroline.

Just then, Caroline heard a screechy wheel rattling and jouncing down the lane. "Why, it's Mr. Lennox!" she said as he drove from the trees. She was glad to see that he'd found his horse and cart.

Uncle Aaron glanced toward the customs officer, and his smile faded. *What's wrong?* Caroline wondered uneasily. Uncle Aaron had been friendly with Mr. Lennox just two days earlier. What had changed?

"You girls shouldn't have stopped," Uncle Aaron told them shortly. "Get on home now."

Lydia sucked in her breath. Caroline said quietly, "We'll get all the chores done, we promise."

As the girls turned away, the customs officer parked and climbed to the ground. Then he marched toward the men resting in the shade.

Mr. Sinclair scrambled to his feet. "Mr. Lennox!" he called anxiously. "I need to report two missing oxen. I fear that a smuggler has—"

"In a moment," Mr. Lennox snapped. "Aaron?"

Before Uncle Aaron could respond, a husky man with a bushy blond beard stepped forward. "Is there some problem?" He spoke with a German accent.

"I just need to speak with Aaron, Mr. Zahn," Mr. Lennox said.

Frowning, Uncle Aaron followed Mr. Lennox a short distance away.

Lydia leaned close to Caroline and murmured, "Papa told us to go."

"Something's happened," Caroline whispered back. "Don't you want to see what it is?" All of the other farmers had gone quiet. They wanted to find out what was happening too.

Mr. Lennox and Uncle Aaron began speaking in low tones. Uncle Aaron shook his head: *No.* Mr. Lennox leaned closer, talking faster, one finger stabbing the air. Both men looked angry.

Behind Caroline, Mr. Zahn muttered, "Do you suppose Lennox suspects Aaron of smuggling? I'd never have guessed *that*."

Then Mr. Lennox's voice rose. "You're right, I have no proof. But if there is proof to be had, I will find it."

Lydia's cheeks flushed. Caroline was sorry she'd forced her cousin to linger. "You were right," she whispered. "Let's go."

Before they could leave, however, Caroline heard someone calling, "Lydia! Yoo-hoo!" One of the women who'd been bundling the cut wheat stalks was making her way from the field. She was plump and wore a kerchief tied under her chin. Her cheeks were red as apples, and she paused to mop her face with her apron. But she smiled broadly at the girls as she approached.

"Good afternoon, Mrs. Zahn," Lydia said.

Mrs. Zahn put her hands on Lydia's shoulders. "Ah, child. It is always good to see you." Her German accent made *good* sound like *goot*. "And who is this pretty girl?" She inspected Caroline with friendly eyes.

"I'm Caroline Abbott, ma'am," Caroline said. "Lydia's cousin. I'm helping out while her mother is away."

After a nervous glance at her father and Mr. Lennox, Lydia explained to Mrs. Zahn about the quilting bee and picnic supper.

"A frolic!" Mrs. Zahn clapped her hands. "I'll be there, and I know my husband and Peter will come to the picnic."

"Would you pass the invitation to the others?" Lydia asked. "Caroline and I really must get home."

"Of course, child." Mrs. Zahn nodded vigorously and hurried away.

Caroline and Lydia left the clearing. Once on the main road, Lydia walked so fast that Caroline had a hard time keeping up with her. "Oh, Caroline, what is happening? What would Mr. Lennox and my father have to argue about?"

"Well . . . they must have been talking about smuggling," Caroline said reluctantly.

Lydia stopped walking. "Papa would never get involved in smuggling!" she insisted. "Never, ever, *ever*!"

Caroline sucked in her lower lip. *I don't blame Lydia for defending Uncle Aaron,* she thought miserably. If someone accused her own papa of smuggling, she wouldn't believe it for a second. But watching Mr. Lennox threaten Uncle Aaron was the worst, most suspicious thing that had happened yet.

Lydia began to walk again. Several minutes passed before she spoke again. "It was hard on Papa to flee Upper Canada when the war began, and to start over here with almost nothing. I know he's worried about that land payment. And I know he came up with some plan that Mama doesn't approve of. But Caroline, my family would rather lose our farm than sell potash to the British!"

Caroline thought again about all the terrible things that had happened to her family and friends and country since the war began. The memories made her feel hot inside. All she could do was nod.

As soon as they got home, Lydia surveyed the cabin's cooking area. "We need to start preparing food for the men's work party tomorrow," she said. Caroline was almost glad they had such a huge meal to prepare. Being busy might keep Lydia from fretting about her father's argument with Mr. Lennox.

Uncle Aaron did not come home in time for supper. After milking, Caroline sat at the table and tackled the plums. A few had worms, so she had to be careful when cutting the fruit into bite-sized pieces for a cobbler. Lydia mixed dough and spooned it over the fruit in the Dutch oven. The girls nestled the heavy cast-iron pot in the fireplace and put hot coals on the lid. "The men will be well fed tomorrow," Caroline said.

"I want to do my mother proud." Lydia looked determined. "Anything less would be a disgrace."

Caroline wished Lydia hadn't used that word, which shoved her thoughts from cooking back to smuggling. *Oh, **surely** Uncle Aaron wouldn't disgrace the family by doing business with the British!* she thought. It had to be someone else. She felt more determined than ever to identify the person making potash in the secret clearing.

The next morning, Lydia and Caroline jumped from bed before sunrise, ready to begin cooking. Neighbor men began arriving at the farm soon after dawn. Most of them came on foot. Mr. Zahn and his son Peter strode into the farmyard with axes propped over their shoulders. Mr. Sinclair rode Snowflake. Caroline hoped that the skittish mare was getting used to her rider.

Lydia and Caroline greeted each arrival politely, as Aunt Martha would have done. Caroline met a few more neighbors. Mr. Skelly bowed low over her hand as if she were a princess, which made her smile. "Since your mother is away, my wife sent some small

cakes along," he told Lydia, handing her a basket.
A Dutch settler named Mr. Aabink spoke very little
English, but with a jolly smile offered a block of
cheese wrapped in cloth. "From my Anna," he said.
Lydia introduced Caroline to a bachelor new to the
area, and an older man who had sixteen children.
"My wife and daughters were excited to hear about
the quilting bee," he told the girls.

Caroline and Lydia exchanged a delighted glance.
"Word is spreading fast!" Lydia said.

"Girls?" Uncle Aaron called. "I'd like one of you
to bring a jug of cold water out to the field every now
and again. Add a dash of cider vinegar—that's the
most refreshing thing on a hot day."

The men got to work in the field. Some chopped
dead trees with axes. Others hauled limbs to the
field's edge to begin building a new brush pile.
Several more set fire to the old pile. *It's a poor morning
to be burning brush,* Caroline thought, for a hot breeze
blew smoke across the field and yard. But this was

the day the men had set aside to help Uncle Aaron, so they'd have to do the best they could.

Several times that morning, Caroline filled a jug with the water-and-vinegar mixture Uncle Aaron had asked for, and carried it outside. Drifting smoke made her eyes water as she walked through the field, offering the jug to each man in turn. Each took a swig, wiped his mouth on his sleeve, thanked her, and got back to work. They covered their mouths and noses with kerchiefs, reminding her of the robbers who'd taken the barrels of salt beef from Mr. Lennox.

"I'd hoped to eavesdrop on the men's conversation," she reported to Lydia back in the cabin. "But they're spread out and working hard. Nobody's talking."

Lydia straightened from the hearth, where she was roasting ears of corn in their green husks. "Try again during the midday meal," she suggested.

At noon, Caroline and Lydia set out a pan of

water and a towel so that the men could wash their faces and hands. The girls used a bench for a serving table and covered the kettles and plates with clean rags to discourage buzzing flies. Once the men filled their plates, they dropped to the ground on the shady side of the cabin to eat, where they could keep an eye on the blazing brush pile.

Caroline gave them a few minutes to get started before approaching with a basket of bread. To her frustration, Mr. Zahn was talking loudly about his pumpkin crop. *Maybe after the embarrassing argument between Mr. Lennox and Uncle Aaron yesterday,* Caroline thought, *nobody wants to even **mention** smuggling.*

All too soon, the men set their plates aside and walked back to the field. "I don't think we're going to learn anything today," Caroline muttered to Lydia as they started stacking the dirty dishes. "I wish . . ." Her words died as Mr. Lennox drove his cart into the yard. "What's he doing here?"

Lydia looked worried. "I hope it's not more trouble."

Once again the customs officer parked beneath a tree and approached the field. Uncle Aaron left his ax and came to meet him. The other men stopped working too. Caroline and Lydia edged closer.

"What is it now?" Uncle Aaron demanded. He pulled off his hat and swiped his face with his arm, leaving a sooty streak on one cheek. "I've no time for idle chat."

Mr. Lennox surveyed the yard with narrowed eyes. "I'm not here for an idle chat."

The other men exchanged uneasy glances. Lydia grabbed Caroline's hand.

Uncle Aaron stepped closer to the officer. "If you have something to say, just *say* it." His face looked like a thundercloud. "I—"

"*Look!*" Caroline cried, pointing behind him as a yellow flicker shot away from the bonfire. More flames, greedy for the dry sticks and leaves left in the field, raced in a different direction. While the men had been distracted by Mr. Lennox, the burning brush pile had flared out of control. Because of the wind, the fire was spreading fast.

Fear squeezed Caroline's heart like a fist. If they couldn't beat back the flames, the whole farm might be destroyed!

chapter 10

Under Arrest

CAROLINE'S SKIN FELT prickly as she watched the men race toward the flames. "Lydia, fetch my shovel!" Uncle Aaron hollered. "And the hoe!"

"I'll get buckets," Caroline yelled. She darted into the cabin and grabbed two pails. Mr. Aabink, who'd followed her inside, snatched them from her and ran out the door. Next, Caroline pulled several blankets from a shelf and dragged them to the door. Mr. Lennox himself pulled the blankets from her arms and plunged them into a nearby rain barrel. Then he ran toward the others.

Caroline stumbled after him. Not sure what to do next, she looked around with stinging eyes . . . and was surprised to see a flash of blue through the swirling smoke. She blinked, and the blue was gone.

Was that Peter Zahn in his bright vest? she wondered.
If so, he was running away from the fire, instead
of helping.

She rubbed her eyes and peered back toward
the others. Peter was nowhere in sight, but there
was no time to wonder about him. Uncle Aaron was
digging frantically, shoveling scoops of earth on
the fire. Mr. Sinclair was helping him with the hoe.
Mr. Lennox and several other men beat flames with
the wet blankets. Caroline heard the wicked crackle
of flames, and the hiss of wet wool.

Lydia was pulling branches and other bits of
deadwood out of the field in hopes of starving the
fire. Caroline ran to help. Stumbling over the rough
ground, she began grabbing sticks and hurling them
with all her might away from the approaching flames.

She was panting and had lost all track of time
before she heard Uncle Aaron say, "There, now.
I think we've got it." Flames still flickered yellow and
orange here and there, but they were sulking now.

"We must keep a sharp eye out," Mr. Zahn called. "A gust of wind could cause another flare-up. Peter, help keep watch."

Peter nodded. He stood nearby with hands on his hips, chest heaving.

Was I mistaken? Caroline wondered. Was Peter breathless because he'd run away from the fire, or because he'd worked so hard to fight it? His face was wet with sweat.

"Mr. Livingston." Mr. Lennox cocked his head toward the cabin.

The two men left the others in the field, and Lydia and Caroline followed. "I'm grateful for your help," Uncle Aaron told Mr. Lennox stiffly.

"You're welcome," the customs officer said, just as stiffly. "But you and I still have business. I've come to search your place for evidence of illegal trade with the British."

Uncle Aaron's jaw dropped with shock. For a moment Caroline thought he would refuse permission. Then he gestured wide with his arm. "Search if you must. You'll find nothing."

Mr. Lennox walked to the cowshed. The family followed as he stepped inside. Caroline and Lydia exchanged an anxious glance. They'd put the coin pouch back on top of the beam where they'd found it. Caroline's stomach flip-flopped as she imagined the customs agent finding the pouch. *It's not illegal to keep money in a shed,* she told herself, but she feared it would only add to Mr. Lennox's suspicions.

Mr. Lennox, though, seemed to decide that it would be difficult to hide anything in the small building. After a quick glance around, he left the shed and walked back across the yard. Caroline's face felt hot as she saw that the neighbor men in the field were all watching.

Mr. Lennox walked through the garden gate. After scanning the rows of vegetables, he approached a tall basket full of food scraps—rotten bits of plums, pigeon bones, corn husks—and kicked it over.

A small leather pouch, tightly tied closed with a thin leather cord, tumbled out with the garbage.

Caroline could hardly believe her eyes. "Why— what—that does not belong to us!" she stammered. She'd tossed some carrot scrapings into that basket and hauled it outside right before serving the midday meal. She knew that the pouch had not been there then.

Mr. Lennox glanced over his shoulder to the watching men. Then he picked up the pouch and looked at Uncle Aaron. "What's this?"

Uncle Aaron stared blankly. "I have no idea."

As Mr. Lennox turned the pouch over, Caroline glimpsed faint letters that had been stamped into the leather—well worn now, but still visible.

Mr. Lennox traced the letters with one finger. "J. M., King's Eighth Regiment," he read grimly. "It appears that this pouch belongs to someone serving in the British army." He undid the tie and looked inside the pouch. Then he poured a stream of grayish crystals into his palm. "This is potash."

"Well, it's not mine." Uncle Aaron crossed his arms over his chest.

The customs agent rubbed his forehead. Then he said, "Mr. Livingston, you are under arrest. You will be charged with making potash with the intent to sell it to our enemy, the British."

"No!" Lydia cried. "It's not true!"

Caroline felt heartsick. When the war began, she'd had to watch a British officer take her own papa away. But Mr. Lennox was not an enemy. In some ways, that made this situation even worse.

"I will come with you," Uncle Aaron snapped, "but only so that we can sort this out. Just give me a moment with the girls."

Uncle Aaron beckoned to Caroline and Lydia to follow him inside. In the cabin, he sat down by the table, and they stood before him. "I don't know what this evil mischief is all about," he said, "but I am sure we can discover the truth."

"Papa—" Lydia began.

"Hush, now." He grasped Lydia's hand, and then Caroline's. "I rely upon you to take care of the farm in my absence. We have many good neighbors, so call on them if need be. I'll be home as soon as I can."

"Uncle Aaron," Caroline whispered, "*are* you a smuggler?" She was horrified as soon as the words popped out. She hadn't planned to ask anything of the sort.

Her uncle leaned closer, holding her gaze. "No, I am not." He spoke slowly, making each word important.

Caroline knew in her heart that he was telling the truth. Relief made her feel trembly. The flickers of suspicion she'd felt all week were finally put to rest.

Uncle Aaron looked at Lydia. "Have faith, daughter. If I'm not home by the quilting party, I want you to go anyway."

"I don't care about the quilting party!" Lydia protested.

"It will do you both good," her father said firmly. "Just lock the cows in the shed if you're going to be away from the farm all day. And I need you to do something for me at the Pembertons'."

"Anything!" Caroline promised.

Her uncle walked to the hearth, grasped the edge of one of the stones used to build the fireplace, and pulled it out. Then he reached inside, removed a small leather wallet, and began counting its contents. Caroline wondered again about the coin pouch still hidden in the cowshed, but this was not the time to ask about it. *If Uncle Aaron hid it there,* she thought, *he had a good reason for it.*

"This is the money I got for selling my watch," he was saying. "Take this"—he pressed several coins into Lydia's hand—"and ask Mr. Pemberton if he has any salt to sell. All right? We need to put up plenty of fish and game for the coming winter, and we must have salt for that."

"Yes, Papa." Lydia's voice quivered, but she

nodded. Caroline was proud of her.

Uncle Aaron returned the wallet and replaced the stone. He went back outside and called the men over. He spoke to them in a low tone.

Then he climbed into Mr. Lennox's cart. Caroline and Lydia stood in front of the cabin, and the neighbor men stood silently, too, as Mr. Lennox drove Uncle Aaron away.

chapter 11

Likely Suspects

MR. SINCLAIR AND the Zahns joined Lydia and Caroline on the front step. "The others have gone," Mr. Zahn said, "but they made sure that every spark is out. You don't need to worry about the fire."

"We're all very sorry about what has happened," Mr. Sinclair added. "Would you like to come home with me? Or have Mrs. Sinclair come to stay with you?" His face looked gray. Caroline hoped that what had happened wouldn't give him another bout of heart trouble.

Lydia glanced at Caroline before saying, "I think we'll stay here."

"I'm sure Aaron will be home again very soon." Mr. Zahn stroked his beard. "If you girls need help with anything, just ask."

"Thank you," Lydia said, with great dignity.

Peter's head was bowed. *Does he feel bad for Uncle Aaron?* Caroline wondered. *Or does he feel guilty about something?* So much had happened in the last few minutes that she'd forgotten about that blue flash she'd seen through the smoke. If it was Peter, just what had he been doing while everyone else was fighting the fire?

Mr. Zahn and Mr. Sinclair mumbled farewells, and the trio left. "Let's go inside," Caroline told Lydia.

Once in the cabin, Lydia sat down and finally let her tears spill over. "Papa's on his way to jail in the village! And it's hard to blame Mr. Lennox after he found that bag of potash."

"You and I were the ones dumping scraps into that basket all morning," Caroline fumed. "Mr. Lennox might as well have accused *us* of smuggling potash."

Lydia made a helpless gesture. "I simply can't imagine where that sack came from."

"I have an idea." Caroline told her about the blue flash she'd seen through the swirling smoke when the fire flared up. "My eyes were watering, so it was hard to see," she admitted. "But it might have been Peter's vest."

Lydia thought that over. "He was running away from the others?"

"Maybe he had that sack of potash in his pocket and panicked when Mr. Lennox arrived," Caroline suggested. "He might have run behind the cabin while the rest of us were fighting the fire. Once he was out of sight, he could easily have tossed that sack over the fence."

"But why would he have brought a sack of potash to a work party?" Lydia asked.

"Well..." Caroline considered. "Perhaps he was going to pass it to someone else. To whoever rows out to meet British buyers."

Lydia stood and began pacing, arms crossed over her chest. "Somebody is making potash on our land,

and somebody put that sack of potash in our basket. But *who*?"

"I don't know," Caroline said, "but it wasn't Uncle Aaron. Lydia..." She hesitated, and then her words came out in a rush. "You were right. I *was* suspicious of your father. But I know he told the truth today."

"I can't really blame you for wondering," Lydia admitted. "Sometimes I had doubts too, although I tried not to. Oh!" She clenched her fists in frustration. "I simply can't make any sense of what's been happening!"

"I can't either," Caroline said. "But we can't prove that Uncle Aaron is innocent of smuggling until we do, so we must keep searching for answers."

Caroline and Lydia had been alone at the farm before, but it was terrible to have twilight come and know that Uncle Aaron was locked up in jail miles away. "Let's sew this evening," Caroline said. "I want to make my pocket." She knew the best thing they could do was keep busy.

They soon had their scraps spread over the table. "It doesn't look like you have enough of that pretty blue to make a pocket," Lydia observed.

"You're right." Caroline moved the cloth pieces around. "But if I use some of these white scraps too, I can make a patchwork pocket."

"Well, that does seem appropriate, since we're preparing for a quilting bee," Lydia agreed.

Caroline was glad to see her cousin settle in to finish stitching the quilt backing. They worked together until full darkness fell and it was time for bed.

The next morning they rose early, ate breakfast, and milked Minerva. "The rest of the chores can wait," Lydia said. "I want to sneak down and check the potash rig."

"Let's take baskets and gather more plums, too," Caroline suggested. "We can make some jam for Flora."

Caroline and Lydia crept cautiously to the hidden little clearing, but once again it was deserted. The hollow log full of ashes was still plugged, and Caroline couldn't find any evidence to suggest that the smuggler had been there recently.

"We should keep checking," Lydia said, "but I don't think we have time to sit here and wait for somebody to show up."

"Besides, now that Mr. Lennox thinks Uncle Aaron is a smuggler, the *real* smuggler is probably afraid to come back here," Caroline said.

Lydia tipped her head thoughtfully. "I suppose you're right. Mr. Lennox might come back to the farm and do a thorough search if he thinks more goods might be hidden here."

Caroline watched a robin hopping along a branch and tried to think what to do next. "It's hard to imagine that Mr. Sinclair is the smuggler. I know he lives just as close as the Zahns, but his health isn't good, and he's so upset about losing his oxen... I just can't picture him sneaking over here to boil potash."

"Me either," Lydia agreed. "Let's walk toward the Zahn farm. We can poke around a bit there. Maybe we'll find something suspicious."

Caroline held up her basket. "If anyone sees us, we'll just explain that we're looking for fruit."

The girls walked downhill until they reached the creek, then turned left. They scrambled along the bank for perhaps half a mile before Lydia paused. "I think we should leave the creek here," she said. "If we walk up the slope, we'll come up behind the Zahn place."

They made their way through the trees, dodging bramble bushes and trying not to trip over roots. Finally Lydia pointed ahead. "See where the woods thin?" she whispered. "That's the back edge of their bottom field."

"What do you want to do now?" Caroline asked.

Lydia's voice was low but fierce. "I want to find proof that somebody else is smuggling, and not my father."

Caroline peered through the branches, making sure that no one was about. "Let's circle around to the far side of the field," she suggested. "We'll come up behind the barn."

Keeping hidden among the trees, the girls pushed on and soon reached the Zahns' barn. The farmyard remained quiet and still.

"All right." Lydia looked nervous but determined. "I'm going to sneak into the barn. Maybe I'll find a whole barrel of potash."

"Well, I'm coming too," Caroline said. "The search will go faster with two of us."

Caroline and Lydia slipped from the woods to the log barn, scurried along the side wall, took one last look at the empty farmyard, and darted to the barn door. But their hopes fell hard and fast.

The barn door was secured with a lock and chain.

Lydia jerked her head back toward the woods, and they raced into the trees. Caroline felt a little breathless, even though she hadn't run far. "Why do you suppose the barn is locked in the middle of the day?" she asked.

"Maybe they've got Mr. Sinclair's oxen hidden in there," Lydia said darkly.

Caroline's eyes narrowed. Was it possible that Mr. Zahn could steal a neighbor's animals and then work beside him, laughing and joking, as if nothing were wrong? It was hard to imagine. "Or maybe he started locking his barn when he heard about Mr. Sinclair's missing oxen, like we did."

"Maybe," Lydia agreed with reluctance. "Especially if the Zahns aren't home today. Well, let's keep going." She picked a path through the undergrowth. "Ouch," she grumbled when a branch whipped back and smacked her. "It's too hot to—" Her voice broke off. They'd unexpectedly come upon a break in the forest. "What's this?"

Caroline studied a path that had been slashed through the woods. Low stumps showed where someone had cut down trees. The trunks had been chopped into smaller pieces, now lying haphazardly as if tossed carelessly aside. "It's a path," she said slowly, "except it's too wide for a regular path."

"Somebody went to a lot of trouble to make this trail." Lydia peered in one direction, then the other. "It starts right at the Zahns' farmyard, but it seems to go east, in the direction that the road would go anyway. Why do so much work?"

Caroline inspected a thick stub where someone had hacked a branch away. "The raw wood hasn't had a chance to weather yet."

Lydia studied the ground, where weedy growth was still green, but crushed. "This trail may be new, but it's seen hard use already."

"Look at this." Caroline crouched and fingered some broken stems. The stalks had been trampled and pressed into the ground. "These are hoofprints! Lydia, someone has driven cattle through here."

"Oh no," Lydia whispered. "Do you think Mr. Sinclair's oxen were driven through here, where they wouldn't be seen?"

"It seems very likely." Caroline glared at the trail. "I believe we've found a smuggler's road."

chapter 12

The Quilting Bee

"THE ZAHNS MUST have cut this trail to drive cattle east to the Saint Lawrence River," Caroline said. "Mr. Lennox told us it was easier to sell cattle there, remember? At least until winter, when the lake freezes and smugglers can travel across the ice."

"This trail is wide enough for a cart," Lydia pointed out. "They could be smuggling kegs of potash or barrels of salt beef, too."

Caroline nodded. "And since Mr. Lennox has started posting deputies along the real road, this may be the easiest way to smuggle things east now."

"Let's see if Mrs. Zahn is home," Lydia suggested. "We can't come right out and ask her about this, but if we start a conversation, maybe she'll let something slip."

The girls continued their circle around the Zahn farm. When they approached the cabin from the front, they saw Mrs. Zahn sitting in the shade shelling peas. "Oh, girls!" she exclaimed. "Why are you out on such a hot day?"

"We're going to pick plums," Lydia said with false good cheer. "But since we were headed this way, we thought we'd stop and see if you were home."

"I'm glad you did," Mrs. Zahn assured them. "Mr. Zahn and Peter went to Sackets Harbor. They had to wait until the work parties were complete, but my husband has been itching to go for several days."

I'll bet that's because he wanted to take Mr. Sinclair's oxen east to sell, Caroline thought angrily. She imagined Mr. Zahn and Peter driving the team through Sackets Harbor and on to meet a British buyer along the Saint Lawrence River.

"Are they shopping?" Lydia asked innocently. "My father and I found prices quite high when we were last in town."

Mrs. Zahn shrugged. "I asked for a bit of coffee, if he can find it. Otherwise, I let my husband decide what we can afford to buy."

"When did they leave?" Caroline asked.

Mrs. Zahn looked surprised by the question. "Well, it was long before first light. I'm an early riser, but they were gone before I was out of bed."

So, Caroline thought, *it's possible that if Mr. Zahn and Peter **are** breaking the law, Mrs. Zahn doesn't even know.*

"Might we trouble you for a drink?" Lydia asked. "We forgot to pack a bottle of water."

"Of course. I've got a fresh bucket inside." Mrs. Zahn beckoned them to follow her.

Caroline was eager to get a glimpse of the Zahn home. The cabin was bigger than Lydia's. It was not crowded with belongings, however, so there wasn't much to see. Certainly no barrels labeled *Potash for the British.*

She tried not to feel disappointed. Since potash could easily be stored in small containers, it would have been astonishing to find some—especially right under Mrs. Zahn's nose! "Thank you," she said politely, accepting a tin cup of cool water.

As Mrs. Zahn and Lydia chatted about the quilting bee, Caroline wandered closer to the hearth. A candlestick stood on the mantel, and a china vase. Holding the place of honor in the center was a framed silhouette picture. The figures of two boys had been cut from black paper and pasted onto a white background.

Caroline had seen silhouettes before. She was always fascinated by the tiny details the artists managed to show with tiny snips of their scissors. "This is beautiful!" she exclaimed.

"Yes." Mrs. Zahn's voice sounded suddenly heavy. "That cutting of my boys was made a few years ago."

"Your boys?" Caroline echoed hesitantly. She'd thought that the Zahns had just one son—Peter.

Mrs. Zahn stepped closer and touched the taller figure with a gentle finger. "My oldest, Carl, joined the army when the war began. He was killed in July 1812, when an American force tried to invade Canada."

"I'm very sorry," Caroline told her.

"It's been hard on everyone," Mrs. Zahn said. "I'm sad, my husband is angry, and Peter is bitter. He and Carl were very close."

After that conversation, Caroline didn't want to ask any more prying questions. She and Lydia said good-bye and were on their way.

They took the road home. Caroline waited until the Zahn farm wasn't even visible through the trees before saying, "Now I don't know what to think. Surely Mr. Zahn would *never* do business with the British after they killed his son."

"It happened before we moved here, so I didn't know." Lydia blew out a long sigh. "It seems we're farther from learning the truth than ever."

Caroline felt the same way, but she would not give up. "Let's think back through what's happened so far," she suggested. "Mr. Lennox seized barrels of salt beef from a smuggler, and the smuggler and his friends stole them back again. Then Mr. Sinclair's oxen disappeared."

"We found the potash rig in the woods," Lydia went on, ticking off items on her fingers. "Someone put a bag of coins in our cowshed, and a bag of potash in our basket of food scraps. Mr. Lennox arrested Papa."

"And finally, we found a smuggler's road leading from the Zahns' place," Caroline concluded.

"What we haven't found is anything that will get Papa out of jail." Lydia looked discouraged.

Caroline kicked a stone from the road. "Mrs. Sinclair told us that the smuggling problem is a disgrace, and I believe she meant it."

Lydia nodded. "She even said, 'What kind of person would profit by selling goods to the enemy during a war?'"

"And the Zahns are grieving for a son killed

in battle," Caroline continued. "But if it wasn't the Zahns or the Sinclairs who set up that potash rig, who could it be?" She thought of polite Mr. Skelly, and cheerful Mr. Aabink, and the other men who'd come to help burn brush at the farm. "It made sense to think about Mr. Sinclair and Mr. Zahn, since they live closest to the potash rig. But maybe that's all wrong."

"It's going to be very hard for me to go to the quilting bee tomorrow," Lydia said crossly. "How can I have fun at a party while Papa's in jail? Especially since one of the guests at the party may be the *real* smuggler?"

"Don't think of it as just a party," Caroline advised. "Once the men arrive, we need to watch and listen as best we can. I can't imagine that Mr. Pemberton is sneaking to your farm to make potash. And *he* should hate the British too, since they stole his ship. Still, since he lives right on the lakeshore, we have to wonder if he's involved in smuggling."

"If Mr. Pemberton *is* trading with the British, he's probably getting rich," Lydia said nervously. "He won't want us to get in his way."

Caroline knew that was true, but she didn't know what else to do. She hated to picture Uncle Aaron sitting in jail. "We'll just have to be careful not to get caught," she told Lydia. Somebody had to find out who was really guilty of smuggling, and she didn't trust Mr. Lennox anymore.

Caroline and Lydia arrived at the Pemberton house early the next morning. They had agreed that it was important to act as normally as possible. Everyone present would know that Uncle Aaron was in jail, but no one must guess that Caroline and Lydia were trying their best to identify *real* smugglers.

Flora greeted them with hugs. "This day is going to be such fun!"

Caroline tried to smile. What would sweet Flora

say if she knew that Caroline and Lydia suspected her father of smuggling?

She struggled to put those thoughts aside as more quilters arrived. Some had come from miles away, leaving home before dawn in their eagerness to attend the quilting bee. Caroline also met the wives and daughters of some of the men who'd come to the work party at Lydia's farm. Mrs. Skelly was a short, red-haired woman with a friendly manner. Mrs. Aabink seemed to speak even less English than her husband, but she approached Lydia with sewing needle in hand. "I help, yes?" she asked hesitantly.

"Yes," Lydia said gratefully. "Thank you."

The women and girls worked together to spread the quilt backing on a quilting frame, which was like a big wooden picture frame held up on posts. Next they placed wool in a thick, even layer on top of the backing. "You girls did a lovely job cleaning and carding this wool," Mrs. Sinclair said.

Finally, they pinned the quilt top in place over

the wool. Mrs. Sinclair passed around the thread she'd spun. Then everyone pulled up chairs around the frame, threaded their needles, and began stitching the three layers together. It would take many rows of tiny stitches all across the quilt to hold the wool in place. *But it won't seem like a big job,* Caroline thought, *since we're all working together.*

The women chatted about their children, their gardens, their embroidery and knitting. No one mentioned what had happened to Uncle Aaron, but everyone was extra sweet to Lydia. Caroline heard Mrs. Skelly quietly ask Lydia if she needed any help at home, and another lady offered to stop by the farm to help with heavy chores. Caroline was touched by their kindness.

Mrs. Zahn sat by Caroline. "How pretty!" Mrs. Zahn said, admiring the patchwork pocket Caroline had finished sewing the night before. It wasn't fancy, but the corners of all the little blue and white squares were sharp and met perfectly.

"Thank you," Caroline said. "I thought I'd wear it outside my skirt today, so my handkerchief and thimble are handy."

At noon, Flora set out bread and jam, pitchers of lemonade, and a plate of small cakes to nibble on. The afternoon passed quickly. They'd made great progress on the quilt by the time a clock chimed four times.

"My father said he'd be home by five," Flora announced. "The other men will start arriving as well. We'll stop for supper then."

Caroline still wanted to prowl about, looking for signs of smuggling, and it seemed wise to do it before Mr. Zahn and the other men came. She stood. "I think I'll take a walk," she said, rubbing her fingers as if they were tired. She looked at her cousin, trying to send a silent message: *Come with me!*

"That's nice," Lydia murmured, without looking up from her needle. Caroline hoped that the excitement of seeing the quilt nearly completed might actually have pushed thoughts of smuggling out of Lydia's mind, at least for a few moments.

Outside, Caroline wandered toward the cove, trying to look carefree to anyone glancing out a window. When she and Lydia had arrived that morning, they'd spotted Deputy Squinty and his companion walking along the water's edge, but they weren't in sight now. Mr. Pemberton's skiff was tied up at the dock. Caroline didn't see any suspicious crates or kegs inside—but since the deputies were patrolling the shore, that wasn't surprising. If the potash maker wanted to row his crystals out to a British ship, Mr. Lennox and his men were making it difficult.

Caroline went next to the barn, which was out of sight of the parlor windows. The two big doors that allowed a man to drive a wagon right inside were closed. Caroline slipped through a regular door in the side wall, shutting it carefully behind her. She paused, letting her eyes adjust to the dim light. The stable smelled of manure and old hay. There were several stalls, each empty.

Mee-ow! A tabby cat popped from behind a row of crates near the far wall.

Caroline stooped and held out her hand. "Here, kitty!" she called. She missed her own cat, Inkpot, who would have come to rub his head against her fingers. The shy tabby, though, ran back behind the crates.

Too bad, Caroline thought. Then, *Oh my—**crates***! Maybe she'd found what she was looking for.

But she'd only taken two steps when she heard the clip-clop of hooves and the rattle of wooden wheels outside. Before she could think what to do, one of the big doors swung open. Light flooded the barn. Mr. Pemberton appeared in the doorway. His black horse and small wagon were visible beyond him in the drive.

Caroline tried not to look guilty. "Good day, Mr. Pemberton."

His brows lowered in a frown. "What are you doing in here?" he demanded.

She thought fast. "I saw a tabby cat. I do love cats, so—"

"Yes, yes," he interrupted. "You run along now."

"Yes, sir." Caroline walked quickly back to the house, wondering if she'd stumbled into an important discovery. Was there something in the barn that Mr. Pemberton didn't want her to see?

chapter 13

Searching for Evidence

BY THE TIME Flora served the picnic supper, twenty or more men had arrived. Mr. Zahn and Peter came, and Mr. Sinclair. Caroline waved at Mr. Skelly, and Mr. Aabink, and the other men who'd helped burn brush at the farm.

Mr. Lennox arrived in his cart, too. Caroline watched with surprise as Mr. Pemberton gave the customs officer a warm welcome. *Maybe Flora's father isn't smuggling after all*, she thought. Or . . . perhaps Mr. Pemberton was being friendly to Mr. Lennox in hopes of throwing off suspicion. Caroline tried to catch Mr. Lennox's eye, but he was quickly surrounded by other guests.

Lydia carried a platter of cold fried chicken outside and placed it on the big plank table set up in the yard. Then she pulled Caroline aside. "Did you see that Mr. Lennox is here?" she asked in an urgent whisper. "Should we tell him about the smuggler's road?"

"There's no harm in reporting what we saw," Caroline said. "Even though I don't completely trust him, since he arrested your father."

"Let's watch for a chance," Lydia murmured. "I also wanted to tell you that Mr. Zahn and Peter had an argument right after they arrived. I wasn't close enough to hear, but Peter stormed off toward the lake."

"Toward the lake?" Caroline tucked that tidbit away in her mind. Then she told Lydia what had happened in the barn. "Flora's father seemed unhappy to see me there."

Flora stepped outside and rang a bell. "Supper will be served in a few minutes," she called.

"Be watchful," Caroline hissed to Lydia. "I will too."

Caroline made herself as helpful as possible during the picnic supper, circling among the guests with jugs of lemonade and bowls of potato salad and platters of ginger cakes. Mr. Lennox was always talking with the other men, and he never glanced her way. Peter Zahn had returned, but she had no way of knowing if he'd simply taken a walk or if he'd been on some darker errand. She didn't see or hear anything helpful, and when she caught Lydia's eye, her cousin shook her head to show that she, too, hadn't learned anything.

Caroline wanted to return to the barn while the guests were still eating supper, but a few of the men stood nearby, passing a flask that probably held whiskey. She couldn't slip into the barn to check the crates she'd spotted without being seen. Instead, she circled around the house and walked past the vehicles parked along the drive. She counted four wagons and five smaller carts. Each was empty. If anyone had taken advantage of this party by the lake to deliver potash or salt beef to Mr. Pemberton, there was no sign of it.

After supper Mr. Pemberton passed cigars to the men, and they stayed in the yard to smoke. As Caroline helped gather up plates and forks, she saw more bottles and flasks being passed among the men. "Say, Lennox," one man complained. "I got stopped twice by deputies of yours on the way here. Do you need to be so bothersome?"

Finally! Caroline thought. She walked more slowly, hoping to hear something new. But, "Just doing my job," Mr. Lennox said mildly. "Sorry for the inconvenience."

The evening passed without Caroline finding a chance to slip back inside the barn. The ladies added a few more lines of stitches to the quilt, but the men stayed outside. A moon rose almost full, bathing the yard with pale light even as daylight disappeared. Finally, women reluctantly began gathering their baskets and calling their husbands.

"This has been a *wonderful* day," Mrs. Sinclair told Lydia and Caroline. "Bless you girls for planning it—and you too, Flora, for having us all here."

The guests trooped out to the drive to say their farewells. Some lit lanterns.

"Wait!" Mr. Pemberton called. "I've planned a toast to send you on your way."

"Sounds good!" one of the men called. His voice was slurred.

Lydia leaned close. "Most of these men don't need anything more to drink," she observed.

Caroline agreed, but Mr. Pemberton was passing glasses of wine to all of the adults. "A few words, if I may." He spoke like a man used to giving speeches. "There is no finer honor than opening my home to my friends..."

Suddenly Caroline realized that this formal farewell was an opportunity. Mr. Lennox was surrounded by other guests, so she couldn't talk with him, but perhaps she could get a peek inside those crates in the barn. "Come on," she whispered to Lydia. "This is our chance."

They silently backed away from the guests. The big barn doors were closed again. When the girls crept inside, the barn was very dark. Caroline walked in what she hoped was the right direction, arms outstretched to keep from banging into something. One hand struck solid wood. A loud snort and the sound of stamping hooves came very close to where she stood. Her heart leapt into her throat before she realized that she'd bumped into Mr. Pemberton's wagon.

"When I saw Mr. Pemberton drive in earlier," she whispered to Lydia, "I assumed he was going to unharness and tend his horse. Instead, the horse is still hitched to the wagon." Her eyes were adjusting to the dim light.

"Was the wagon loaded before?" Lydia murmured. "It is now."

"Mr. Pemberton made me so nervous that I didn't

notice," Caroline admitted. She studied the wooden wagon box. Something bumpy was hidden beneath a sheet of canvas.

The canvas was lashed down so tightly that she couldn't peek over the side of the wagon. She made her way to the rear and unlatched the back panel, which lowered to make loading easier. She reached under the canvas. Her hand met the hard, rough side of a wooden crate . . . and another, pushed against one side of the wagon bed. She could feel more crates against the other side.

Caroline dearly wanted to know what was inside those containers! Outside in the yard, Mr. Pemberton was still speaking, his voice drifting faintly into the barn. "Keep watch," she advised. "I want to see what's hidden in this wagon."

"All right, but hurry," Lydia whispered anxiously. "No—wait! Flora is calling me!"

"You go find Flora," Caroline said. "If she asks for me, tell her I followed the cat into the woods."

Lydia scurried away. Caroline lifted her skirt and crawled into the wagon, under the canvas covering. There was a narrow gap between the crates. Just in case someone else wandered in, she pulled the back-board up again and latched it closed.

Then she ran her hands over the wooden boxes. To her frustration, the lids were nailed shut. She fingered the sides of a crate, feeling the gaps between boards, but the cracks were too narrow for even her pinkie finger to poke through. In desperation she pressed her face against one of the gaps and inhaled. The faint, meaty smell of bacon reached her nose. The crates held pork! And meat was one of the things Mr. Lennox had said the British wanted to buy.

*This isn't **proof** that Mr. Pemberton is smuggling,* Caroline thought. But why else would he be hauling crates of salt pork in August? Meat spoiled quickly in hot weather, and she'd never known anyone to butcher hogs before the first frost. The British, though, had enough hungry sailors and soldiers in

Upper Canada to eat the pork before it spoiled.

She became aware of rising voices outside, saying their good-byes. Mr. Pemberton had finished his speech. He and Flora would wave each wagon and walker on their way, but then he would surely come to unhitch his horse. She needed to return to the party, *now*.

Caroline tried to wriggle backward, but her skirt snagged on something. She didn't want to rip it, so she fumbled in the tight space, trying to find the spot that was caught. Finally she managed to free herself from a splintery board. She reached back for the latch that would allow her to lower the backboard again— but she heard something and went still. Had someone come into the barn? She held her breath.

The wagon lurched. Someone was climbing to the driver's seat!

Caroline heard the slap of leather lines. "Git up there," a man muttered, *very* close to her. The horse began to walk. The big barn doors must have been opened, for the wagon rolled from the smooth barn floor and rumbled onto the drive.

I have to get out of this wagon! Caroline thought. She reached again for the latch, but one wheel jolted into a rut and she fell back against the crates. The wagon kept moving down the drive. She heard another horse nicker, and the creak of other wooden wheels, and pictured other guests climbing into their carts and wagons and forming a line. Everyone would drive down the lane to the main road, where some would turn east and some would turn west.

She didn't know what to do. Should she yell to the driver and make him stop? But how would she explain why she was hiding in the back?

Almost immediately, the wagon jerked to a stop. "Halt!" called a familiar high voice that could only belong to Deputy Squinty. "None of you may continue until we've searched your wagons."

"You've no cause to bother us!" a man yelled angrily.

"You have spent time here along the lakeshore," Deputy Squinty retorted. "That's all the cause we need."

Then Mr. Lennox's voice rose above the others. It sounded like his cart was right behind the wagon Caroline was riding in. "Let us through, Jim. I've been with these fine men all evening." He sounded happy, as if he'd had a bit too much whiskey. "There are no smugglers here."

"Why—Mr. Lennox!" Deputy Squinty stammered. "Sorry, sir. I didn't see you there."

"Safe travels, my friends," Mr. Pemberton called from behind them.

Caroline felt more confused than ever. The guests had parked their vehicles outside, so she'd assumed that the horse and wagon she'd found shut into the barn belonged to Flora's father. If he wasn't driving her wagon, who was?

Clip-clop! Clip-clop! The horse began to trot. She heard other horses and wagons ahead and behind as the guests left the Pembertons' drive and turned onto the lane that led south, one after another. If she squeezed through the gap between the wagon bed and its canvas cover, and tumbled into the road, she might get trampled.

Panic flared beneath Caroline's ribs. She was in big trouble.

chapter 14

Answers—and More Questions

WHERE ARE WE GOING? Caroline wondered. Without knowing who was driving, she couldn't even guess. All she knew was that every turn of the wheels took her farther from Lydia and Pemberton Cove.

In the tiny space beneath the canvas covering, she was bumped and banged as the cart jounced over the rough lane. Finally she managed to brace her feet and arms against the wooden crates. That helped a little.

Before long, she felt the wagon turn onto the main road. *Where are we* ***going***? Caroline wondered again. She still had no idea how to escape the wagon without getting hurt—and being seen. Every passing minute made her more anxious. Finally she began counting in her head. It helped to have something to do.

She'd gotten to six hundred and seventy-three when the driver suddenly muttered, "Whoa." The cart veered, then stopped. Caroline felt the lurch as the driver—she still hadn't recognized the low voice, although it sounded like a young man—climbed to the ground. Her heart began to skitter beneath her ribs again. Was she about to be discovered?

The cart that had been right behind them rumbled to a halt as well. "You folks got trouble?" Mr. Lennox called.

Yes! Caroline wanted to yell, but she kept still.

"Just a loose axle on the wagon," a man called from the road ahead. Caroline recognized Mr. Zahn's accent. He must have been driving in front of her wagon, and had pulled off the road and stopped as well.

"I'd be glad to give you a hand," Mr. Lennox said.

"No need," Mr. Zahn called. "My boy and I can handle it."

The words echoed in Caroline's head. *My boy?* Was Peter the one driving her wagon?

"Suit yourself," Mr. Lennox said. Caroline heard the customs officer's cart drive away. *Should I have called to him?* she wondered. It was too late now.

Footsteps came closer—it sounded as if more than one person was approaching. Mr. Zahn spoke again. "Peter, do you think Lennox got a look inside that wagon?"

"No," Peter said, very close to Caroline's hiding spot. "I kept an eye on him the whole evening."

It sounded as if Peter had been driving Caroline's wagon. He didn't have a German accent like his parents. *But I've never heard him speak before,* she realized. No wonder she hadn't recognized his voice when he spoke to the horse.

"Good thing Lennox likes his whiskey," Mr. Zahn was saying. "If he hadn't tossed a few back tonight, he might not have ordered those deputies of his to let us all pass. Now that he's ahead of us, we can just drive on home."

"Do you have a brain in your head?" a woman asked sharply, just as close. If not for her accent, Caroline would never have recognized Mrs. Zahn's voice. She had always sounded so sweet and good-hearted!

"There could be another roadblock just around the bend," Mrs. Zahn continued. "We'd be fools to carry that load of salt pork any farther."

Mr. Zahn muttered a few German words before continuing in English: "Perhaps we should have left the pork back at the cove after all."

"I said as much!" Mrs. Zahn retorted. "It's always safer to get crates straight onto a British ship than to haul them about New York."

"The boss said that too many customs officers are watching the shoreline right now," Peter said, with some heat in his voice. "Especially around Pemberton Cove."

"He'll tell us when it's safe to use the lake again," Mr. Zahn added, "but that probably won't be until we get a hard freeze this winter and can travel on the ice."

Caroline felt a fierce sense of triumph. *I have proof!* she thought. *I can swear to a judge that I heard the Zahns talking about smuggling.* Now, if only she could find out who "the boss" was ...

"I am beginning to think that he does not have the stomach for this business after all," Mrs. Zahn was saying. "Perhaps you should stop working with him."

"How can I?" Mr. Zahn snapped. "I don't know who the British buyer is. I don't know his schedule. All I can do is what I'm told. And I was told to drive the pork east tomorrow on the hidden road."

"What feeble excuses!" Mrs. Zahn sounded disgusted.

"Stop arguing!" Peter begged his parents.

Mr. Zahn ignored his son. "You got us into this

dangerous business in the first place, wife. And now you still aren't satisfied? Hush. Peter and I will figure out what to do."

"Don't you tell me to hush!" Mrs. Zahn cried. "The British killed our son. Should we struggle and starve now, or make them pay? I will squeeze every cent I can from them. Taking their money is the only way we can get revenge."

"That's not true," Peter retorted. Now he sounded as angry as his parents. "I want to *fight* them, but you won't let me go."

"Do you want to bring your mother even more grief?" Mr. Zahn demanded. "You will stay home and help me with the farm."

Caroline imagined Peter's scowl when he said, "I don't care about the farm!"

"One of those customs men could come back here at any time and find us with a wagonload of salt pork," Mrs. Zahn snapped. "And you two are arguing about farming? You'll land us all in jail!"

"We are not going to jail," Mr. Zahn said. "We'll just hide the crates of pork in the bushes here, and come back when the customs men are snoring in their beds, and—where are you going?"

"I am walking home!" Mrs. Zahn's voice sounded fainter already.

"You will do no such thing!" Mr. Zahn protested.

Peter said, "Mama, wait!" at the same time.

Fading voices and footsteps suggested that the Zahn men had followed Mrs. Zahn as she marched away. *Now is my chance*, Caroline thought. She shoved her head and arms through the narrow gap between the canvas cover and the wagon's tailboard and pushed off with her feet. Despite clenched teeth, a whimper of pain escaped as she landed in a heap behind the cart. She dusted off her hands and strained her ears. The Zahns were still arguing some distance away. No one had heard her.

She was able to see quite clearly in the moonlight. She crept farther from the two parked wagons.

Mr. and Mrs. Zahn had been driving their big
farm wagon. The smaller wagon Caroline had been
trapped in surely looked like Mr. Pemberton's. *If it
is, then Flora's father **must** be involved too,* Caroline
thought. *Is he "the boss"?*

She was crouched out of sight behind a tree some
distance away when the three came back. Mrs. Zahn,
who had evidently decided not to walk home after
all, gave orders while Mr. Zahn and Peter unloaded
the crates of salt pork and hid them in the woods.
Then the Zahns climbed back into their vehicles and
drove away.

When she was sure they were gone, Caroline
began trudging back toward Pemberton Cove. Poor
Lydia was no doubt frantic with worry by now.
Caroline wasn't sure she could face Mr. Pemberton,
who almost certainly was a smuggler. *But he has no
idea what I just overheard,* she reminded herself. She'd
have to pretend that nothing had happened until she
had a chance to tell Mr. Lennox about the Zahns.

She walked along the edge of the road. *Thank heavens for the moon on this clear night,* she thought. Still, it was spooky to be out all alone. "Stay steady, Caroline," she whispered. She tried to memorize the conversation she'd overheard, so that she could repeat it to Mr. Lennox.

She was relieved to reach the junction with the lane leading to Pemberton Cove. Then a loud rustle erupted from the undergrowth nearby, and a man stepped into her path. "Ooh!" she squeaked.

"Halt!" he said at the same time.

Caroline put a hand over her racing heart as she recognized Deputy Squinty. "You frightened me!" she said.

The second deputy walked from the woods with a lantern in his hand. He must have had it hidden behind a screen of some kind.

"Please," Caroline began, "I need to—"

"Who are you?" Deputy Squinty demanded.

"I'm Caroline Abbott," she said impatiently.

"We met two days ago, remember?"

"Are you all right, child?" the other man asked more gently. "Why are you wandering alone at this hour?"

Caroline wanted to tell her tale to Mr. Lennox directly. "Please, sir, if you could just let me pass, I'd be ever so grateful. I was at a quilting bee at the Pemberton house all day, and I—I got lost in the woods. My friends must be very worried."

"What are you carrying?" Deputy Squinty asked.

"*Nothing!*" Caroline felt close to despair. Couldn't he see that she had no basket over her arm? Then she realized what he was staring at. "You mean my pocket? There's nothing in it but a needle case and some thread and a handkerchief. See for yourself." She untied the strings and handed the pocket over.

Deputy Squinty held her pocket close to the lantern. He checked its contents quickly, but stared longer at the pocket itself. He fetched a leather satchel from behind a fallen log and studied something Caroline couldn't see. Then, to her astonishment, he dropped her beautiful patchwork pocket into his satchel.

Before she could protest, he grabbed her arm in a tight grip. "You," he said coldly, "are carrying illegal goods."

Caroline stared at the man in astonishment. "I . . . *what*?"

"Fetch my horse," Deputy Squinty told his friend. And to Caroline, "Thank you, Miss Abbott. You have given us even more evidence that Aaron Livingston is a smuggler." He smiled a mean smile before adding, "And you are coming with me."

chapter 15

Back to Pemberton Cove

CAROLINE DIDN'T KNOW where Deputy Squinty planned to take her, but she didn't want to go. With a mighty twist, she yanked her arm free from the deputy's pudgy fingers. She lifted her skirt and ran into the woods. The tall man had walked to the left to fetch his horse, so she ran right.

She hadn't taken more than a few steps when the shadow of another man appeared from behind a tree. He grabbed her arm, just as the deputy had done.

"Let me *go!*" Caroline shrieked.

"Miss Caroline, be calm," the man said urgently. "It's Mr. Lennox."

Being captured by Mr. Lennox did nothing to make Caroline feel calm. This man had arrested Uncle Aaron, and now his deputy wanted to arrest *her.* "I haven't done anything wrong!" she cried, trying to wriggle free. "And neither has Uncle Aaron."

"I'm trying to help your uncle," Mr. Lennox said. Keeping his iron grip on her arm, he led Caroline back to the deputies in the road.

"Why—it's— Sir!" Deputy Squinty stammered. "I thought you'd traveled on to—"

"I gave the impression of traveling on, and then I circled back," Mr. Lennox said. "I left my cart a short distance away." Caroline realized that his voice was no longer slurred. She didn't smell any strong spirits, either. Usually the drunken sailors she passed on the street in Sackets Harbor reeked of whiskey.

"Now," the customs officer continued. "What's all this fuss with Miss Caroline?"

"Please, me first," Caroline said quickly, afraid she might not get another chance. She told Mr. Lennox about the potash rig and the smuggler's road that she and Lydia had discovered in the woods, and about crawling into Mr. Pemberton's wagon. She ended by repeating the conversation she'd overheard between Peter and his parents. "So I am *certain* that Mr. Zahn and Peter are smuggling meat," she concluded.

"Miss Caroline, you have helped a great deal," Mr. Lennox said. "I had wondered about the Zahns, but I had no evidence. Thanks to you, now I do."

"I didn't hear the name of the man they're working with, though," Caroline said with regret. "I think the one they call 'the boss' usually rows meat or other goods to the British. It must be Mr. Pemberton, don't you think? I'm pretty sure it was his wagon loaded with salt pork that Peter was driving."

"It's possible," Mr. Lennox allowed.

"Now that you've set deputies to patrol the lakeshore," Caroline continued, "perhaps Mr. Pemberton decided it was too dangerous to use his skiff. Instead, he sent those crates of salt pork on the main road with the Zahns."

"May I speak, sir?" Deputy Squinty shifted his weight back and forth impatiently. "This young lady hasn't said anything to prove her uncle's innocence. In fact, I suspect she is trying to cast blame on others so that her uncle will *look* innocent."

"That's not true," Caroline protested.

Deputy Squinty ignored her. "What she hasn't told you, sir, is that I caught her carrying British goods."

"I am *not*!" Caroline insisted. Deputy Squinty made her furious.

The deputy produced her patchwork pocket and handed it to Mr. Lennox. "The cotton here was manufactured in England, sir. This blue flowered pattern matches one of the samples you gave us this morning from that British merchant ship our men seized."

Caroline felt as if all the air was sucked from her lungs. "It . . . it does?"

Mr. Lennox looked at her. "Where did you get this pocket, Miss Caroline?"

"I made it myself," she told him. "But I got the blue cloth from Flora."

"Let's go visit the Pembertons," Mr. Lennox said.

He instructed his deputies to remain at their post.
Then he fetched his cart. Caroline climbed to the seat
beside him, and they started down the road toward
Pemberton Cove.

Since she'd wanted a chance to talk to Mr. Lennox,
she was glad he'd left the deputies behind. "Sir? What
did you mean when you said you're trying to help
Uncle Aaron?"

"He asked me to keep this a secret," Mr. Lennox
said, "but I think you deserve an answer. The evening
when I had dinner with your family, he and I talked
while we did chores. Aaron didn't want to get involved
with the smuggling problem, but he was so desperate
for work that he asked if I needed another deputy."

"Did you hire him?" Caroline asked.

"Not officially," Mr. Lennox explained. "We
agreed that he'd help patrol the lakeshore while
pretending to be hunting. I hoped he might spot the
smuggler I saw earlier, heading out to meet a British
boat. But the smugglers are clever. They change the

rendezvous points and times. They muffle their oars to make it difficult to hear them rowing after dark. Sometimes they paint their boats black, so they can disappear against the night."

"So that's why Uncle Aaron spent a whole day hunting without finding much game," Caroline said.

"That's why," he agreed. "Although I must say, you girls have produced more information about the smugglers than either he or my deputies did."

Caroline hoped he'd tell Deputy Squinty as much.

"Your uncle and I also planned a fake argument at the Zahns' work party," Mr. Lennox continued. "We thought that if his neighbors saw us, anyone who *was* smuggling might think they could trust him. He didn't expect you girls to be there, though, and he almost refused to go through with it."

Caroline remembered how happy Uncle Aaron had been to see them—and how as soon as Mr. Lennox arrived, his smile had disappeared and he'd tried to send them home. *He wanted to spare our feelings,* she realized. She looked up at Mr. Lennox. "What about finding the sack of potash at our farm? Was that fake too?"

"No," he said soberly. "We'd planned for me to stop by, as if I were keeping an eye on the place, but I was shocked when I actually found that potash! And I could tell that Aaron was just as shocked. Since it had British markings, I had no choice but to make a show of arresting him. Once we left your farm, we put our heads together and decided to let things play out in hopes that I could find the real smuggler once and for all."

"How did you plan to do that?" Caroline asked.

"Well, I talked Aaron into staying out of sight for a few days," Mr. Lennox explained. "He's been patrolling another stretch of lakeshore for me at night—that's where he is now. His help meant that I could attend the Pembertons' party. I pretended to get drunk, putting everyone else at ease. And that wasn't hard, because Mr. Pemberton seemed *very* eager for me to drink this evening. He handed me two drinks for every one he passed to the other men. I knew he was up to no good. And when I saw Peter drive out of the barn with a wagon full of *something*, and join the line of guests leaving the party, I figured he must be carrying illegal goods."

"But..." Caroline was confused. "When you told your deputy not to search the wagons, you let Peter drive Mr. Pemberton's wagon full of salt pork right past him!"

"That's true," Mr. Lennox said. "I *suspect* that Mr. Pemberton is a smuggler, but I don't have proof. I hoped that if I acted as though I wasn't even thinking about smuggling tonight, Mr. Pemberton might feel safe enough to row a boat out to meet a British buyer after I left. I had another deputy hidden in the woods by the cove, keeping an eye out for anyone trying to row toward Upper Canada."

Caroline nodded. It was a good plan.

"I had more deputies stationed about a mile down

the main road," Mr. Lennox added. "I intended to follow the Zahns until they reached that search point. I thought we could arrest them there, without so many other people around. Otherwise, I might have been overpowered."

Caroline remembered the day she'd traveled to the farm, when the men who'd hidden their faces stole back the barrels of salt beef that Mr. Lennox had seized. "Is that why you didn't search the two wagons when the Zahns pulled over by the side of the road?" Caroline asked.

He shrugged. "It was three of them against me. That was a fight I couldn't win."

They were approaching the Pemberton place now. Flora and Lydia hurried to meet them, lanterns in hand. Lydia sagged with relief when she saw Caroline. "Oh, thank goodness."

"We were terribly worried about you, Caroline," Flora added, looking equally relieved. "Did you get lost in the woods? Are you all right?"

"I'm fine," Caroline assured them.

Mr. Lennox climbed from the cart and stepped forward. "Miss Flora, may we come inside? I'd like to ask you and your father a few questions."

She looked startled. "My father is still out looking for Caroline," she told him.

Mr. Lennox took a few steps away. He had two pistols, and he fired each one into the air. Caroline knew that anyone searching for a lost child used that signal to let other searchers know that all was well. She was sorry she'd worried everyone.

"Thank you," Flora told Mr. Lennox. "I'm sure my father will be along soon. Now, please do come in." She led them all into the kitchen. "The quilting frame leaves no room to sit in the parlor," she explained.

They all took seats around the table, and Mr. Lennox held out Caroline's patchwork pocket. "Miss Flora, Caroline tells me that she got this blue flowered cloth from you. Did your father buy it for you? If not, where did you purchase it?"

Flora fingered the pocket, as if trying to remember. Then she shook her head. "I didn't buy this cloth, and my father didn't either. I'm not sure where it came from. I love to sew, and I often trade scraps with other women."

"I see." Mr. Lennox sat back in his chair, eyes narrowed thoughtfully. "Well, it is indeed late, so I'll be on my way." He stood and politely nodded. "Miss Caroline, will you walk me out?"

Caroline waited until they were outside before grabbing Mr. Lennox's sleeve. "Please, sir, you can't give up!"

"What can I do?" he said wearily. "If Miss Flora says she doesn't remember where the cloth came from, I can't prove that she's lying. And actually, I think she's telling the truth. I've had a lot of practice watching guilty faces."

"But Flora will wonder why you asked about the blue cloth," Caroline said.

"Give her an honest answer," Mr. Lennox told her. "It won't hurt for people to know that I'm keeping an eye out for British cloth. Also, you can tell your cousin that her father is *not* in jail and will be home soon, although I do ask that you both keep quiet about the details." He sighed. "Now, I'll go send one of my deputies to look for those crates the Zahns hid, and I'll stand watch. There's always a chance that someone might risk a trip to the lakeshore."

Caroline plodded back inside, struggling against rising frustration. They had gotten some answers tonight, and they were very close to getting more! But they had been stopped short.

She returned to the kitchen. "Caroline, what is all this about?" Lydia demanded.

"Mr. Lennox says that blue cloth was made in Great Britain," Caroline told them.

"Truly?" Flora looked horrified.

"Truly," Caroline said. "That's why he wanted to know where you got it."

"Oh my." Flora knelt by the hearth and began to lay a fire. "I think I'll make a pot of tea."

Caroline watched as Flora placed two large logs carefully and crisscrossed smaller sticks on top. Then she reached into a nearby basket and pulled out a handful of something that looked like bits of old twine.

Lydia and I saw that same stuff at the Sinclair place, Caroline thought. For her tinder, Flora was using the tangled scraps and broken bits of stalk left after flax fibers were cleaned. When Flora touched a burning candle to the dry bits of flax, they flared up immediately.

"Flora?" Caroline asked. "I noticed that you used scrappy bits of flax to start the fire."

"Mrs. Sinclair gives me sacks of that waste, so I don't need to make tinder," Flora told her.

Caroline frowned, wishing she weren't so tired. She'd seen a pile of those scrappy bits of flax some-where else, too . . . hadn't she? She thought hard, and finally the memory slipped into place.

And then another memory. And another.

She jumped to her feet and grabbed Lydia's hand. "Flora, please excuse us," she said quickly.

"What?" Flora looked astonished. "Where are you going in the middle of the night? If you must go, at least wait until my father can take you home!"

"Lydia and I need to catch Mr. Lennox and talk to him about something," Caroline said. "I'm *terribly* sorry to be so rude. I promise to explain everything as soon as I can. But right now, we have to leave."

chapter 16

A New Suspect

LYDIA WAITED UNTIL they were outside before protesting. "Caroline, what—"

"Please listen," Caroline said, tugging her cousin down the moonlit road. She described everything that had happened since she'd crawled into the wagon. The best part was explaining that Uncle Aaron was *not* under arrest. "He'll be home soon," she concluded.

"I'm so happy I could cry," Lydia said. "But why are we running after Mr. Lennox now?"

"Just wait," Caroline said, "so I only have to explain everything once."

Before too long she spotted the customs officer's horse and cart parked beside the lane and a shadowy figure sitting on a log. "Mr. Lennox?" Caroline cried. "It's me, Caroline Abbott!"

Mr. Lennox scrambled to his feet. "Why—"

"I figured it out!" Caroline announced.

"Miss Caroline, it's quite late," Mr. Lennox said. "You girls really should not be—"

Caroline couldn't help interrupting. "I think Mr. Sinclair is making potash!"

"What?" Lydia gasped. Mr. Lennox rubbed his chin.

Words tumbled out as Caroline described the rough flax fibers Flora had used for tinder. "I saw the same stuff by the woodpile near the potash rig. No one else around here grows flax."

Mr. Lennox shook his head. "I can't accuse Mr. Sinclair of smuggling just because you found some flax fibers, Miss Caroline."

"There's more," she insisted. "The Sinclairs used to live on the Saint Lawrence River, right on the border. He likely knows lots of people in Upper Canada. He might be 'the boss' the Zahns spoke about!"

"I need evidence, not wild guesses," Mr. Lennox

said. "And remember, Mr. Sinclair lost his team of oxen, almost certainly to a smuggler."

Caroline's mind was racing. "Well, perhaps he didn't actually lose them." She looked at Lydia. "He'd been out with them all morning, remember? In a field that Mrs. Sinclair can't see from the house. It's possible he led them down the creek, past our place, and then on to the Zahn farm."

Lydia nodded as she realized what Caroline was suggesting. "Maybe he heard how high the price for fresh beef is right now and couldn't resist. He sold them to the Zahns, and the Zahns drove them east on their new road."

"Mr. Sinclair keeps a ledger book in his barn," Caroline said. "Isn't it more likely that a man would keep record books in the house? But Mrs. Sinclair hardly ever goes to the barn. Mr. Sinclair might keep his records there if he didn't want his wife to see them, right?"

"Hmm," Mr. Lennox murmured.

"You said the men who row goods out to British ships muffle their oars," Caroline pressed on. "Well, I saw two very long, narrow sacks made of wool in the Sinclairs' barn. At first I thought they might be used to hold potash, but they were damp, so I figured I was wrong. But they'd be the perfect size to fit over oars."

Mr. Lennox stared blindly at the black forest. Then he shook his head. "I just can't see it. Mr. Sinclair is not a young man."

"And Mrs. Sinclair says he has trouble with his heart," Lydia added soberly.

"She also said he sometimes leaves the house to hunt at night," Caroline countered.

"I suppose any man strong enough to plow with a team of oxen is strong enough to row out to a ship," Mr. Lennox said slowly. "But I doubt that Mr. Sinclair is the boss of anything. Smuggling must just be a summertime occupation for him. Driving across the frozen lake in the bitter cold of winter is dangerous!

A man could freeze out there. And unlike Mr. Zahn, Mr. Sinclair has no son to help him. Is there any evidence that Mr. Sinclair might actually be planning to drive goods across the lake this winter?"

Caroline was sure she was on to something, and she didn't want Mr. Lennox to tell her—*again*—to leave the smuggling problem to him. She hesitated, thinking hard.

Suddenly Lydia caught her breath. "There *is* evidence," she gasped. "Snowflake!"

"Of *course*," Caroline said, understanding at once. "Mr. Lennox, the Sinclairs used to have a lovely, calm horse called Bess. Mr. Sinclair just sold Bess and bought a nervous horse named Snowflake. Mrs. Sinclair misses Bess, and I wondered why her husband made the trade. But Bess was dark, and Snowflake is white. Wouldn't it be helpful for a man wanting to travel over the frozen lake in secret to use a white horse who'd blend in with the snow?"

"Hmm," Mr. Lennox said again. He was silent for

a long moment. The night was so still that Caroline heard the rustle of some tiny creature through the leaves beside the road, and the beating of her own heart.

Finally Mr. Lennox nodded. "None of this is proof," he cautioned. "But when you add everything up . . . I agree, it's worth investigating. Let's go hear what Mr. Sinclair has to say."

It must be late, Caroline thought when they reached the Sinclair farm. In the moonlight, the cabin was dark and still.

That didn't keep the customs officer from banging on the door. "Mr. Sinclair?" he called. "It's Mr. Lennox. I need to talk to you."

A few minutes later the door opened. Caroline and Lydia followed Mr. Lennox inside. The Sinclairs had lit several candles. In the dim light, Caroline saw that both had hastily dressed.

"Has something happened?" Mrs. Sinclair asked anxiously.

"I'm sorry to disturb you at this hour, but it couldn't wait," Mr. Lennox said. "May we sit down?"

"Of course," Mr. Sinclair said, but his voice quavered.

Once everyone was seated, Mr. Lennox explained all of the evidence Caroline and Lydia had discovered.

Mrs. Sinclair sat very straight, with a growing look of indignation. "How dare you?" she demanded at last, frowning at Mr. Lennox. "We would never—"

"*We* would not," Mr. Sinclair interrupted. "But *I* did."

"What?" his wife gasped.

Mr. Sinclair patted her hand. "I'm sorry, my dear."

She snatched her hand away. "What have you done?"

"I have bought goods from a few of our neighbors and sold them to the British," he said simply. "I was supplied with a rowboat, which I keep hidden near Pemberton Cove. When I have meat or potash, I tie a white cloth from a certain tree as a signal." He leaned over, elbows on knees. "I traded Bess for Snowflake so that I could haul goods over the lake this winter. And I sold my oxen to the Zahns, who drove them east."

Although Caroline's suspicions had led them here, it still shocked her to hear Mr. Sinclair's quiet confession. *Maybe deep down I wanted to be wrong,* she thought.

"Did you also make potash yourself?" Mr. Lennox asked. "The girls discovered a potash rig on the Livingstons' land."

"No." Mr. Sinclair spread his hands in a weary gesture. "I suppose I should tell you everything. I did help Peter Zahn set up that potash rig. He desperately wants to buy a musket and join the army, but his father won't permit it. Peter decided to make potash in secret and cut that clearing in the woods. But the poor boy didn't actually know how to make potash.

He'd heard that I was a smuggler, and he asked if I might help him get started and then sell his potash crystals."

"Did that leather pouch Mr. Lennox found at our farm belong to Peter?" Lydia asked.

"I'd given it to Peter," Mr. Sinclair admitted. "He filled it and planned to pass it back to me after the work party. When he saw Mr. Lennox arrive, he panicked and tossed it away."

I suspected as much, Caroline thought.

Mr. Sinclair gave Lydia a beseeching look. "Neither one of us *ever* intended for your father to get into trouble."

Lydia nodded shortly. Caroline could tell that she was quivering with anger. She could also tell that Mr. Sinclair was very sorry that Uncle Aaron had been accused of smuggling.

Mrs. Sinclair had listened with a growing look of horror. "Why have you done such terrible things?" she demanded of her husband. *"Why?"*

"Because I am not a well man," Mr. Sinclair said. "And I am terrified by the prospect of leaving you alone and penniless, my dear wife."

Mrs. Sinclair closed her eyes for a moment. Then she asked, "Why didn't you talk with me about this? We would have found another way!"

"I could see no other way," her husband said. He looked at Mr. Lennox. "We have no children, you see. Who will care for my wife if I am gone? How will she manage? Every cent I have made is stored safely away for her use."

The room grew quiet. Caroline felt a salty lump rise in her throat. Lydia's eyes were glistening.

Mr. Lennox rubbed his face with his palms. Then he said, "I appreciate your honesty, Mr. Sinclair. But now I must arrest you for breaking the law."

chapter 17

Home Again

TWO DAYS LATER, Caroline and Lydia were picking corn in the garden when Mr. Lennox drove into the yard—with Uncle Aaron on the seat beside him. "Papa!" Lydia shrieked. She and Caroline ran to greet the men.

Uncle Aaron leapt down and pulled both girls into his arms. "I'm glad to be home," he said. "*Very* glad."

Lydia invited Mr. Lennox to stay for supper, and they all went inside. Caroline had caught two trout in the creek that morning, and Lydia built up the fire so that she could roast them.

"Mr. Lennox?" Caroline asked as she began to mix a batch of cornbread. "Is Mr. Sinclair in jail?"

"He is," the customs agent told her. "Mr. and Mrs. Zahn and Peter are as well."

"It's hard to imagine Mr. Sinclair and the Zahns in jail," Lydia said quietly. "They've helped us out many times."

"We have other good neighbors," Uncle Aaron pointed out.

Caroline thought about the Aabinks, who didn't speak much English but looked for ways to help others. She thought about kind Mr. and Mrs. Skelly, and the other friendly people she'd met at the quilting party. *Uncle Aaron and Lydia still have lots of friends*, she reminded herself.

"I heard that Flora Pemberton has invited Mrs. Sinclair to stay with her for the time being," Uncle Aaron added, "so she's not alone."

Caroline was grateful for that. But she agreed with Lydia—it was hard to imagine someone like Mr. Sinclair in jail for smuggling. Not long ago, she'd believed that there could be no good reason for any American to trade with the enemy. The situation had seemed simple: There was right, and there was wrong. It was like the difference between good and bad, black and white.

But it isn't always so simple, she thought. She wished it were! But there were lots of shades in between black and white. And sometimes there was something in between right and wrong. She still hated smuggling, but she didn't hate the Sinclairs or the Zahns.

"What about Mr. Pemberton?" she asked. "Did Mr. Zahn or Mr. Sinclair tell you about anything that involved him?"

"No," Mr. Lennox said. "But I suspect that Mr. Pemberton *is* involved. It's very possible that when the war began, Mr. Pemberton *sold* his sloop to the British, along with all the goods he'd packed into the hold. The British would have paid him more than what the sloop and trade goods were worth. Then he came home claiming that his ship had been stolen."

"Now, *that* picture makes me angry," Uncle Aaron growled. "Mr. Pemberton was well-to-do before the war began. If he's trading with the British, it's just because he's greedy."

"I have no proof," Mr. Lennox said. "But I'll keep searching." He looked from Caroline to Lydia. "You girls identified four smugglers. That will keep lots of meat and potash out of British hands."

"And *that* will help end the war," Uncle Aaron added. "Which is more important than anything else."

Talk turned to other things, and they enjoyed a companionable supper. Then Mr. Lennox said it was time for him to go. "Thank you," he said to Caroline and Lydia. He paused, rubbing his chin. "I would never have guessed it, but you two made fine deputies."

Mr. Lennox's praise made Caroline feel good. She and Lydia exchanged a grin as the customs officer left the cabin.

"I owe you girls an apology," Uncle Aaron said, when the three were alone. "Worry about losing the farm made me short-tempered. I'm sorry."

"There's still something I don't understand," Lydia said. "We found a sack holding a few coins in the shed. Is it yours?"

Uncle Aaron looked surprised. "You found that?"

"I saw you slip out to the barn that night," Caroline told him. "The next morning, while I was trying to figure out why, I noticed the pouch string. It had slipped over the beam where you hid the pouch."

"The money you found is an advance payment from Mr. Lennox," Uncle Aaron explained. "If I'm 'going hunting' more often, I need to buy more gunpowder. I actually hid the pouch out there because I was afraid you'd find it in here!"

"I wish you'd just told us that you were working for Mr. Lennox," Lydia said.

Uncle Aaron sighed. "Trying to stop smugglers can be dangerous business. Your mother didn't want me to work for Mr. Lennox at all. In the end, we agreed that we should keep my work a secret so you wouldn't worry."

Lydia took a deep breath. "Papa, your secret just made us worry *more*. We knew that something was wrong, but we didn't know what."

"I wanted to protect you," Uncle Aaron said mildly. "Sometimes I forget how much you both have grown up lately. Do you forgive me?"

"Of course!" Lydia gave him a hug.

"Of course," Caroline echoed. She hugged him too.

"So," Uncle Aaron said. "Did you finish the quilt?"

Lydia beamed. "We did! I'll go get it." She retrieved the quilt from the loft and spread it out on the bed.

Caroline considered their creation. It was sewn with light colors and dark colors and every shade in between. Mrs. Zahn's stitches were in that quilt, and for a moment Caroline wished that weren't so. Then she decided that she didn't mind. Mrs. Zahn had helped make the quilt because she'd wanted to do something nice for Lydia. That was all that mattered.

"I like your quilt very much," Uncle Aaron declared. "It's pretty."

"It's cheerful," Lydia added.

"It's perfect," Caroline said. "Perfect for your new home."

Lydia looked anxiously at her father. "Papa? The farm is safe now, isn't it? Now that you're working for Mr. Lennox?"

"Yes," he told her. "The money I earn will let me make the land payment and buy the supplies we need for the winter. I'll save anything left over toward buying an ox. Then things will get easier."

Caroline smiled. She knew that even with an ox, building this farm would still be challenging. But for the first time in a week, she saw the Uncle Aaron she'd always known—hoping for the best, and ready to work hard to make a home for his family.

She let her thoughts drift back over the road she'd traveled from Sackets Harbor. *Her* home was that village, where breezes blew and Lake Ontario beckoned and the sky went on forever.

Being at war was a terrible thing, but she and Lydia had helped bring war's end a tiny bit closer. *You won't beat us,* she silently told the British. *We are Americans, and we are here to stay.*

Inside Caroline's World

Growing up along the border with Canada, Caroline would have heard a lot about smuggling. Her home in Sackets Harbor is right on the shore of Lake Ontario, the boundary between New York and the British colony of Upper Canada. Trade between the United States and Britain had once been perfectly legal. Trading ships crisscrossed the lake, and families like the Abbotts sailed to the British port of Kingston to shop. But all that changed as tensions grew between the two countries.

In 1807, the U.S. ordered citizens to sell goods only to other Americans and buy goods only if they'd been made in this country. The law was meant to prove that the U.S. was strong and independent, and to create hardships for British colonists used to buying American supplies.

Instead, the law hurt Americans. It was much easier and cheaper for New York farmers and shopkeepers along the border to trade with buyers in Upper Canada than to haul their goods to any U.S. city. Many decided to ignore the law and smuggle their goods north. Once war broke out, however, Caroline hoped that Americans would stop selling supplies to the British, who were now the enemy. Unfortunately, the smuggling problem got even worse!

Smuggling paid better than ever once the war began.

The British were desperate to feed all the troops now stationed in Upper Canada, so they paid very high prices for food. Smugglers cut secret roads, like the one Caroline and Lydia discover, through the forests so that wagon-loads of supplies and herds of cattle could be smuggled north to the enemy.

Smugglers could make even more money selling *potash*—the crystals left behind when water is poured through wood ashes and boiled down. Farmers produced lots of ash as they burned trees to clear fields. And English factories needed potash to make cloth and gunpowder.

Customs agents like Mr. Lennox tried to stop the flow of supplies to the British, but their job was nearly impossible. Many people hated the law that prevented trade, or they sympathized with farmers struggling just to survive. Customs agents were threatened and attacked, just as Mr. Lennox is. And if smugglers *were* arrested, sympathetic judges sometimes set them free. Even some community leaders smuggled openly. Jacob Jennings Brown, a local businessman, was such a well-known smuggler that he became known as "Potash Brown."

As Caroline discovers, wartime forced many people along the border to make complicated and painful choices.

Read more of CAROLINE'S stories,
available from booksellers and at *americangirl.com*

⇝ *Classics* ⇜
Caroline's classic series, now in two volumes:

Volume 1:
Captain of the Ship
When war breaks out and Papa is captured, Caroline must learn to steer a steady course without him.

Volume 2:
Facing the Enemy
The war comes closer and closer to Sackets Harbor. Can Caroline make the right decision when the enemy attacks?

⇝ *Journey in Time* ⇜
Travel back in time—and spend a day with Caroline.

Catch the Wind
Go sailing with Caroline, help raiders capture an enemy fort, or ride an American warship to a hidden bay! Choose your own path through this multiple-ending story.

⇝ *Mysteries* ⇜
Enjoy more thrilling adventures with BeForever characters.

The Jazzman's Trumpet: A Kit Mystery
A valuable trumpet goes missing! Can Kit prove *she's* not the thief?

Secrets in the Hills: A Josefina Mystery
Could legends of ghosts and treasure really be true?

A Growing Suspicion: A Rebecca Mystery
Who is jinxing the Japanese garden where Rebecca volunteers?

Danger in Paris: A Samantha Mystery
Samantha and Nellie discover a dark side to the "City of Light."

A Sneak Peek at

Catch the Wind

My Journey with Caroline

Meet Caroline and take an exciting journey
into a book that lets *you* decide what happens.

I run outside, slamming the door behind me. Now that I've left the air-conditioning, the air slaps my skin like a hot, damp towel. I run across the lawn and plunge down the path that leads through the woods to the pond.

This has always been my special place. It's shady here, and quiet. I plop down on the grassy bank, bring my knees up, bury my face in my arms, and cry.

I haven't cried this hard since I was little. As little as the twins, maybe. Thinking of them makes me angry all over again. I haven't heard Mom tell *them* that they have to do extra chores while she's away serving on a navy ship. I haven't heard Dad tell *them* that they have to be extra brave. It's not fair.

After a while I run out of tears. I raise my head and wipe my eyes. My breath is all shuddery and my nose is running.

"Would you like a tissue?" Mom asks quietly. I hadn't heard her following me, but now she sits down on the bank too. I wipe my eyes and blow my nose. "I'm sorry this is so hard on you," she says.

"*Ple-e-e-ease* don't go away!" I beg.

Mom's mouth twists sideways like it does when she's thinking. Finally she says, "Sometimes it helps to talk. Can you tell me what you're afraid of?"

I've never told Mom that I'm afraid, but she's smart about guessing stuff. I'm bursting to say, *"Everything!"* I have to clench my teeth to hold that word inside.

It's true, though. I'm afraid I won't have time to do *anything* except help Dad with the twins. Even worse, I'm afraid I'll miss Mom so much that I'll be miserable every single second of every single day. I'm afraid Mom will get hurt. Worst of all is imagining her sailing away. Those navy ships are huge, but still puny compared to all the water in an ocean.

Mom gently brushes my hair from my forehead. "I don't *want* to be away from my family for so long, you know," she says. "I'll miss you every minute."

"Really?" I ask.

"Really," Mom says. "But I'm also proud to serve

my country. My father served in the navy, and his father before him. It's a chain of service that hasn't been broken for over two hundred years! I want to carry on that tradition. And I want to make the world a safer place for you and your sisters," she adds quietly. "I need you to be brave. Can you do that for me?"

I am positive that I won't be able to do that. I wish I *were* brave, like Mom. But I'm not.

Mom says, "I want to give you something." She holds out her hand with fingers curled over the gift.

She's got a present for me? I hadn't expected that, and I feel a teensy bit better. Mom and Dad have promised that I can get my ears pierced on my next birthday. Maybe she picked out special earrings for me!

What she gives me isn't a little jewelry box, though. Instead, my present is round and hard and made of metal. A piece of glass protects a dial on one side.

I glance at Mom. "Um . . . is it a pocket watch?"

"No," Mom says. "Take a closer look."

There are only a few letters on the dial: N, NE, E,

SE, S, SW, W, NW. Now I get it. "You're giving me a compass?" I ask, totally confused. What's the point in having a compass when you can use GPS?

"I'm giving you a very old compass," Mom explains. "My father gave it to me when he was shipping out for a voyage at sea. He got it from his father, and so on. This compass goes back to the very first person in our family to serve in the navy. That was during the War of 1812."

I can tell that Mom thinks I should be excited about this, but honestly, I wish a pair of sparkly earrings had gotten passed down in my family instead.

Mom gives me her *This is important* look. "Sailors in our family have always used this compass to navigate. I hope it will help remind you to steer a steady course while I'm at sea." She closes my fingers over the compass. Then she gets up, kisses the top of my head, and starts walking back to the house.

After a moment I lie down and wriggle to the edge of the bank. I see my reflection in the still pond below.

My eyes are all red and funny-looking from crying.

I hold the compass in front of me. The gold part is dull and dented, and the glass is cloudy. What am I supposed to do with it?

I turn the compass in my hand, but the needle on the dial keeps pointing in the same direction—north. Right now, it's pointed straight at me. The needle looks like a little arrow aimed at my heart. I think about how Mom going away *feels* like an arrow in my heart.

Suddenly I see movement in the water below. My reflection is trembling, as if someone had tossed a rock into the pond. The water ripples and sloshes until my face becomes a blur. Feeling dizzy, I close my eyes, the compass clutched tight in my hand.

After a moment the dizziness passes. I open my eyes. The water is still, and I can see my reflection again.

Except... it's not me.

I blink. The face I see in the water is mine, but I'm wearing an old-fashioned bonnet. This morning I put on a bright red T-shirt with sequins, but now I seem to be wearing something pale blue with white lace around the collar. And instead of the pond's muddy bottom, I see stones through clear sparkling water.

That's so spooky that I scramble to my feet, tripping because that pale blue top is actually a long dress.

Gulping, I look around. The summer heat is familiar, but that's all. Instead of the little pond, I'm beside a humongous lake that stretches into the distance.

What is going on? I feel dizzy all over again.

"Are you looking for warships too?"

I whirl around. A blonde girl about my age is walking toward me, easily making her way over the stones. She's wearing a long pink dress and looks as if she belongs in a play or something.

I open my mouth, then close it again. Finally I stammer, "Did—did you say *warships*?"

The girl looks out over the lake and clenches her fists. "They're out there," she says. She looks half angry and half scared. "We drove them off yesterday, but they'll be back."

I don't like the sound of *that*. "Um ... who, exactly?"

"The British, of course!" she exclaims. "Those black-hearted British will repair their ships and sail back across Lake Ontario again."

Back to *where*? "This might sound stupid," I say, "but can you tell me where we are, exactly?"

She looks startled. "Why ... you've reached Sackets Harbor, New York. The village is just beyond the curve of the bluff." She grins, and the worry is gone from her face. "My name is Caroline Abbott. Who are you?"

Her smile is so nice that I can't help smiling back. I introduce myself. "And I just arrived," I add, to help explain why I have absolutely *no* idea what's going on.

"So you don't know about yesterday's battle," Caroline says. "British ships formed a line in front of Sackets Harbor and fired cannonballs at us! It lasted for hours."

My jaw drops. Have I really and truly landed in the middle of a war? *Oh, Mom,* I think, *I wish you'd stayed with me back there by our pond!*

"But our gun crew fired back," Caroline's saying proudly. "And I helped!" Since she's just a kid, I can't imagine how she was able to help a gun crew. Before I can find out she asks, "Have you traveled far?"

That almost makes me laugh, even though it isn't funny. "Yes," I say again. "Very, very far."

"Are you traveling by yourself?" She looks behind me, as if expecting someone else to appear.

I look around too. We're standing on a narrow strip of stony shore. A rough rock wall, all drippy with moss and ferns, rises straight up behind us. No one else is in sight. "Yes," I tell her. "I'm alone. And I guess I... well, I sort of got lost."

"Now that war has been declared," Caroline says, "lots and lots of people are traveling to Sackets Harbor." She sighs. "I think eighteen-twelve is going to be a very difficult year."

Eighteen-twelve? I seem to have traveled over two hundred years back in time!

About the Author

KATHLEEN ERNST grew up in Maryland in a house full of books. She wrote her first historical novel when she was fifteen and has been hooked ever since! Today, she and her husband live in Wisconsin. Her books for children and teens include the series about Caroline Abbott and many American Girl mysteries. Kathleen's books have been nominated for the Edgar® Award and the Agatha Award, the nation's top awards for children's mysteries.